C000178450

THE LEGEND

THE LEGEND

MARIE BRONSARD

Translated by Sonia Alland

LONDON NEW YORK CALCUTTA

This volume is published through the
Tagore Publication Assistance Programme,
with the support of Institut Française en Inde,
Ambassade de France en Inde.

Seagull Books, 2013

First published in French as *La Légende*

© Domens, Pézenas, France, 1999

English translation © Sonia Alland, 2013

ISBN   978 0 8574 2 102 9

British Library Cataloguing-in-Publication Data
A catalogue record for this book is available from the British Library.

Typeset and designed by Seagull Books, Calcutta, India
Printed and bound by Maple Press, York, Pennsylvania, USA

For Hubert
the younger brother, who died
26 September 2000

With my deep appreciation for Marie Bronsard's collaboration in the translation of this text.

Sonia Alland

THE LEGEND

What a miserable little thing is, from now on, stretched out there, thin, inert, the eyes open but lifeless, the face, a mask fixed in an absent smile. She sings to herself most of the time, repeats monotonous vowels that roll off the tip of her tongue and, with an empty look, laughs at the angels, or perhaps at strands of memories that unravel from the past. One would like to believe it. One would so wish for a link, no matter how obscure, how spare, that would keep her bound to this world, to what was her life. At times, her body arches abruptly, her eyes roll back. Then, she belches out a roar of consonants, prey to an irrepressible violence, to a fathomless anger or to an archaic fear, it's impossible to know.

She is demented. But she is no longer dying. That is to say, not for the present. The course of her destiny seems arrested by the immense void which has spread within her. Save in rare moments of sudden rage, nothing remains of what she was but an envelope of flesh, a body devoid of desire, of pleasure, that abandons itself to the deceiving respite of sleep.

She can no longer speak but still has a voice, no longer perceives but has sight: she lowers her eyelids when the light is too harsh. Hearing, she never really had. She was threatened with silence from childhood.

That's it perhaps, the secret wound which lingers in her mental chaos, the pain buried under the false gaiety that, from time to time, is revealed by outbursts of insane ill temper: the measure of her deafness and its ransom.

In the past, she used lips to guide her and made a show of laughing when she misunderstood, or got angry, depending on the circumstances, her mood or the nature of the person speaking to her. Because of her youth, then her maturity, she had remained beautiful, transforming into charm what she rejected as an infirmity. Playfully, and with a hint of condescension, she accepted the inept compliments that men, troubled by her nonchalance, gave her. In the labyrinth of sound where she moved slowly, and with grace, the walls were a tapestry of mirrors, men's eyes reflected her image.

Late in life, fallen, defeated, she withdrew into herself, was excluded from conversations. She reserved her attention for the one closest to her, for the last of her companions. When, wanting to speak to her, I'd take hold of her arm, she would glance at me with a weary look. She had given up talking. She had given up understanding. On occasion, she'd still launch into long diatribes, pursuing her interior monologue, with no regard for who listened. After that, she would again sink into an obstinate silence. Only her eyes, brilliant, alive, before the glazing over from the cataracts, betrayed her. She was living in a dream without form, without remorse, but with so many regrets.

I see her again in that photograph—the one I asked for but that no one could find. The end of the thirties. At Cape Saint Jacques, in Bien Hoâ or in Saigon, I have no memory for places. And they have little relevance to my story. She's wearing white slacks, floating loose on her narrow hips, and a belted jacket with short sleeves. She's leaning against a motorcycle, next to her first husband. She's beautiful, striking, with dark eyes and hair. How many of her children are already born? Her daughter, obviously. Perhaps also the son, so loved. As for the third one, nothing could be less sure. She seems too radiant to have endured the annoyance of this unwanted child. It was only as she grew older, and when this second son had become an adult—if in fact he ever did!—that she decided to love him.

I no longer remember if, in this particular photo, she was smiling. Nor if he was. Undoubtedly. One posed for photos rarely at that time, but it was always with the thought of leaving a flattering image for posterity. Therefore, very probably, they were smiling.

He's Francis. He's as round as she is slender. He has a frank look and a jovial expression. His face is ageing, his hair thinning. Yet he's not even thirty, or just barely. Five years at most remain for him to live. He's unaware of it.

He's not wearing his uniform. We can't see his rank. In any case, I wouldn't have known how to decipher it, unwilling from early on to understand the cabalistic signs of the military.

Francis detested the army. He detested the debt that, through none of his doing, he'd contracted with it. A widow's son, orphaned of a father he'd hardly known— a soldier sacrificed, like so many others, on the altar of the Great War—he had undergone the lot of all the orphans of his generation: ward of the nation, a child of the troops, military man, future cannon fodder.

But in this photograph it's obviously not a question of war. It was in the limbo of childhood that he'd lived through the Great War. The one that, ripening, far away, in old Europe, he'll not survive.But he knows nothing of that. For the moment, he's proud, as proud of his wife as of his motorcycle, proud of his clothes and of his rather unflattering leather helmet, happy with this beautiful holiday, perhaps satisfied as well with his relatively comfortable means—to which the motorcycle bears witness—the only advantage that, indifferent to marks of esteem, he acknowledges he owes to his enrolment in the army, means which permit him to live in a vast residence and to offer himself, he, the little peasant from the depths of the provinces, the service of domestics. Proud, too, without a doubt, of his two or three children, placed at the moment under the authority of the cook, Bep, and in the care of their personal maids, Ti Aï, Ti Bâ . . . The third one's name I don't remember.

To tell the truth, I don't remember a thing. I wasn't born yet. All of it was related to me. The photograph, on the other hand, I actually saw. A long time ago. Who will tell me, now that the last to remember has no memory, the name of the person who was behind the camera? Wasn't it Jean, even then?

In this photo, next to this beautiful, striking woman, his wife, he does not seem to recall that if he, Francis, finds himself there, on an excursion at Cape Saint Jacques, in Bien Hoâ or near Saigon, far from old Europe, thousands of kilometres from his native Périgord, it's because he tried to flee from this same beautiful woman before she was his. And because he failed.

They'd met in a small city in the centre of France. How? I wouldn't be able to state with certainty. The legend began only after the conception of their first child, a girl. At a dance, I suppose, since, if not dashing—he seems never to have had an imposing physique—he was at least a young and brilliant non-commissioned officer, and she was old enough to go to dances. Old enough also and, above all, most eager to marry, to escape the harsh authority of distant relatives who were exploiting her shamelessly. She laboured in this city where he was stationed, the godchild—or, rather, the servant, taken away barely pubescent from her country—of a Majorcan grocer who had made money in the orange trade.

Up to the end she denigrated where she'd come from. She asserted she was French, in spite of a pronounced accent, which, inaudible to her ears, for her, did not exist. The perspicacity of those who guessed she was foreign always disconcerted and, often, wounded her. She then felt obliged to display her passport. Feeling insulted, she affected an air of scornful dignity—which only partly hid a secret rancour—to proclaim: 'And twice a war widow!' This passport, which was her pride, and glory, was with her constantly in the last years of her life, even when she went out on errands.

Retired, she returned to her island but found life tedious. She liked to evoke Paris at length, the store, the Trois Quartiers and the rue de Rivoli, for her, the bastions of eternal France. She congratulated herself for having frequented distinguished people whom her misfortune and her passion for stone—for concrete, rather, but we'll come back to that—had led her to serve. Out of self-respect, and because the word had a pretty ring to it, for those lending ear, she had attributed to herself the function of 'lady companion', one more flattering than that of 'maid', the position she really occupied. Nasty gossip claimed that, during a period of his sad widowerhood cut short by death, she had kept her old employer very close company indeed. She couldn't bear solitude, it's true, and didn't hide it, but I doubt she committed the irreparable—even though, for some time, she was no longer naive—with a ninety-year-old who shook and was close to senile.

I remember meeting her once when she was passing by, alone, on the Champs-Elysées. She adored the two words joined together, which, for her, held almost as much glamour as the place itself.

Her last companion would often tease her when he'd see her grab hold of her bag. He could never tell if she were going to shop or return to Paris—for her, it was never a question of a short stay or a trip but of an actual return, as if to her native land. This last companion, no more than we, has the heart to tease her now

That day, she scolded me about my skirt being too long and my hair untied. I should, she said, pay attention to my appearance, to how men's eyes passed over me, without stopping, clear proof of my lack of appeal. I was not yet twenty, and the businessmen on the Champs-Elysées appeared most decidedly to be in a hurry. She proposed taking me to the Trois Quartiers, a store she considered the height of distinction because, in the past, her illustrious employers shopped there. She was determined to buy me a simple, grey suit which would flatter my figure and which, because of its classical cut, its fine cloth, I could keep for years. The offer was generous, but I laughed. She wasn't insulted. She only deplored my apparent inability to adapt to the imperatives and rigours of existence. As if to support her observation, she told me a few things in confidence. Life hadn't been easy for her, I was not unaware of that. She had lost two husbands, almost a third one, dead just before he was to marry her—and it wasn't the ninety-year-old. She knew better than anyone the innumerable traps and humiliations that awaited women who were alone, defenceless and without money. She'd had that kind of painful experience. Lowering her voice, she confessed that she'd just taken on a new companion. I smiled, tenderly, without a touch of irony. She then glanced at me in a surprising way, mischievous, as if I were her accomplice. I understood the nature of the secret I was holding. And without hypocrisy, with a sincerity that approached complete candour, she pointed to the sum of misery, sadness, troubles and solitude that her husbands had spared her. And with the same frankness, she listed all the advantages she had reaped: respectability, security, ample pension payments—twice a war widow!—and several houses. Because I showed scepticism as to the necessity of shortening my skirts and tying back my hair to accomplish all this and because, moreover, I contested, in general, the usefulness of wedlock, she was disheartened. The blood in my veins was not speaking up. My future seemed precarious indeed.

Well, Francis, when she was in full bloom and—at least as I imagine it—not yet practiced in feminine guiles, had seduced her, then had become frightened and turned away. What did he fear? Her desires? Her ambition? Her deafness? Her nonchalance? Her immeasurable self-assurance? Or nothing more than his responsibilities? Given his definitive absence, no one can be sure. But the legend is plain: two years his senior, she'd known what it was to be a woman for some time, though she was perhaps unaware of her obligations, in every detail; he, without thinking, had discovered his manhood.

He avoided her. She pursued him. He disengaged himself. She hung on stubbornly. He fled from her. She found him again. She expected reparations. He denied the possibility of his paternity. Did he already have reason to doubt her fidelity?

Having tried everything else, he resolved upon asking his command to expatriate him to some far-away place. To escape this stubborn Majorcan's pursuit, Europe's latitudes seemed too close and Africa still too much of a neighbour. He requested Asia, Siam, Laos or Cochinchina, for lack of one of those outposts in India—with seductive but unpronounceable names—at least, he hoped, for her—that he saw in his dreams. They deferred to his request, the times lent themselves to it. A post in Indochina was soon granted him. He had almost finished packing his bags.

And that's one of the culminating points of the legend, which contains several of them. Warned—How? By whom?—of the wicked deed being secretly planned in the barracks, she raised a scandal. She marched to headquarters. She accosted an officer, a sergeant, for all I know, perhaps a lieutenant. When she was angry, no obstacle could withstand her. She lost all modesty or pride. Nothing, no one, could stop her, restrain her.

Once I saw her force her way into a ministry—the orderly, worn down by her indomitable deafness, finally let her go by—to lay siege to an office until she obtained the hearing she demanded where, under duress, the official granted her husband (the second one) the privilege she, by mistake, considered he'd been unjustly denied. That day she provoked both my embarrassment and my admiration, in that order.

In the earlier event, the legend relates, she assembled the battalion. Proclaimed her misfortune. Cried out the injury done to her. Demanded compensation. La Grande Muette* had never been treated, it seems, to such an uproar. And the unfortunate Francis, ordered to justify his actions, acknowledged his offence. He gave way. He married her.

That's the legend's report. Not her confession.

It had even become a game. As she'd had little schooling and though she claimed to shine in her language, her native tongue, a Catalan dialect which was not written—but all of us respected her pride, pretending not to notice the clumsiness with which she penned her name to the bottom of official forms or in her cheque book—we lent her our savoir-faire, we filled out her papers. And the French bureaucracy furnished them generously to the 'twice a war widow!'

The game consisted of showing astonishment at the closeness of two dates, that of her marriage and that

---

* All words with asterisks refer to a list of terms which, with their explanations, may be found at the end of the volume.—Trans.

of the birth of her first child. With the most complete seriousness in the world, she responded by incriminating either her daughter, born prematurely, or an official who was distracted or, one could even say, ill-intentioned: it was in September and not, as indicated, in December that she was married. Depending on which lie she'd choose, we would demand details about the premature birth, about which we feigned no one had ever told us, or we'd vigorously encourage her to rectify the error which, without doubt, was a wrong that had been done to her. She didn't see the fun we were having—she would have been deeply offended. The affair would end suddenly, with her declaration that she was tired. She'd close her eyes, throw her head back, her mouth half open, her lips quivering. It was clear that she was about to faint. Stifling our laughter, we grew silent.

The fact was that, by nature, she was as much of an actress as a liar. In an embarrassing situation, she was not above fainting. But as long as she had a chance of accomplishing her ends, she made use of lies without scruple. She excelled in the art of illusion. It was probably due to this faculty that she survived the various disasters of her existence. The only problem was that she never remembered the precise content of her previous lies. And it scarcely mattered to her, so long as she considered herself temporarily saved from a bad turn of events.

It was impossible to outwit her. Confuted, unmasked, she'd be overcome by a malaise. Strangers were alarmed, those who knew her well were amused, but everyone signed a truce.

With regard to our game, since with the passage of time the choice of calling the dates an error had prevailed—more convenient or believable in her eyes—we had given up teasing her. The routine repetition of the lie was no longer of any interest.

But no one, not even her daughter, having become a woman herself, then a mother, then a grandmother, could ever force her to reveal the truth.

When I close my eyes, it seems to me I see all three of them aboard the liner that's slowly drawing away from the dock. He's fastened into an impeccable white uniform, even though it's already autumn, but they're heading for more tropical shores. Is she proudly holding her daughter, a few months old, in her arms, as in a later photo she'll display, like the Madonna with Child, her son, the beloved one?

The scene would be idyllic, but we have our doubts about it. She will feel a rush of tenderness for this same girl fifty-eight years later, on the threshold of the abyss that was about to engulf her reason, surrendering her body to the current until it was cast up, extenuated, on a makeshift bed from which it would not rise again: 'If I'd known, I would have loved you long ago.' Already the words of a madwoman, unfettered by a sense of duty or decency, which plunged like a knife into the heart of the one I'm incapable of consoling.

In truth, she loved, and with passion, only two people in the world: her first son and her second husband. To the point of, as time passed, sometimes confusing them. The first son fled to another continent more than twenty years ago. No one has heard from him since. The second husband died more than thirty years ago. She would have so wanted reality to obey her desire, serve her confusion and, in finding the first one again, see the second one once more. Fate did not grant her this happiness, nor this disillusion.

Were the son to return now, she wouldn't recognize him. I want to believe, in spite of it all, that something would tremble in her, a shiver of joy would pass through her of which she'd be unaware but which would bring peace to her body and deliver it from terror as death drew near. She waited for him for such a long time. She dreamt so often of embarking on a ship to search for him. Curiously, she never considered taking a plane, though she didn't lack courage or endurance and was perhaps not fearful of this form of locomotion.

But didn't she refrain from acting, contemplating instead an unlikely and costly cruise, because she feared being disappointed? Or worse?

Her son, to be sure, had disappeared before. Still, taking into account the time that had elapsed and the violence preceding it—one day, pushed too far, he had dared raise his hand to his mother, he'd not been able to bear it—this recurrence resembled a definitive break more than temporary flight.

Already in his last years of adolescence, he'd attempted to escape her, fleeing the country. But the young man, inept—and somewhat presumptuous—had left a trail:

two or three postcards, of inappropriate eloquence, addressed to the sweetheart he'd left behind, the close relative, as luck would have it, of a too-close neighbour. His mother, out of spite, had been informed of the situation. And, in the family's interest—that is to say, in hers alone, the younger brother, the older sister caring not a fig, disdainful even—as for the stepfather, this maternal frenzy was not altogether to his liking—she'd asked that a search be made. A consulate had found him and, as his papers weren't in good order, the authorities had expelled him. He never forgave her for it.

So, when he'd stolen away once more—but she had no idea up to what point this second disappearance was complete, irrevocable—she didn't dare start again. And the inept young man, this time, proved to be more cautious.

No one really knows where he is, if he still resides on that other continent or if he ever made his way there. For my part, I've never trusted those providential witnesses who've claimed to have seen him here or there. It doesn't cost much to assure a distraught old woman that her son is alive and happy and prosperous. With all impunity. Or out of simple kindness. Perhaps, more lucid than we imagine, she'd understood that and preferred shutting her eyes. She knew perhaps that at the end of her voyage she would learn the truth: her son had never gone to that continent, which would mean the end of her illusions. Or worse: that he'd been buried there. Perhaps that's why,

17

year after year, she put off her project, pointing out the expense of the cruise and its infrequency.

It's possible that I'm mistaken, that, all to the contrary, it was from nostalgia, from superstition, that she persisted, in spite of all the difficulties, to imagine this demanding voyage, dreaming of an odyssey that would have ended in a triumphant reunion. She would have resisted the sirens of renunciation, would have just barely escaped the enchantment of despair, would have pierced the vigilant eye of doubt, in a fashion, paid in advance, with her person, in order to attract the restive favours of destiny.

Or, more secretly, was she hoping to undergo a perilous ordeal, defining good sense, putting herself in the hands of the elements?

Or, more simply, did she hope, in the course of her travels, to revisit her past, refreshing as she went from one port of call to another—the island of Ceylon, perhaps, or the coast of Malabar, she so loved to evoke these places, to pronounce these names—a memory that was growing ever weaker, former ports of call where, on route to Saigon, returning to Marseille, she was radiant, splendid, an opulent Occidental, an admired woman, a respected wife, a gratified lover, an adored mother, at least by the most fractious of her three children. Ports of call she presumed, right or wrong, to be the same for a cruise to Australia in our present-day as for a crossing to Indochina in years gone by.

She'll no longer be going aboard. It's too late. And she's no longer waiting for him. Or perhaps she is. Perhaps the expectation alone, indefinite from now on— like hunger, pain and anger—gives her body the force to set its back against the urgent claims of death.

It is that love, excessive, poisonous, abusive, exerting itself to the detriment of everyone, of everything, of decency itself, that separated them. A love ill-fated for them both. She would have suffocated him. Or he would have killed her. Of the two, he, disappearing from sight, would prove to be the wiser. Rather than accuse him of a wrong, we should thank him for it. And he, wherever he is, should bow before the immeasurable sorrow that his exile, deliberately chosen, and his silence, perpetually renewed, has inflicted on his ogress of a mother.

The story goes—but it's the result of nasty gossip and not the legend—that this son can't be attributed to either husband, not the first nor the eventual second. It's murmured that the father might be a distant cousin—in a whisper: the proof, a vague resemblance—whom she would have met upon returning to her island to improve her health.

She adapted very badly, in fact, to the humid heat of the tropics which made her anaemic. And her young junior officer of a husband, temporarily lodged in the barracks, had not found, at first, a properly appointed place for her to live. Initially, she was not granted the stylish life that would distract her from the afflictions, from the boredom of her exile. Thus, in those years separating her sons' coming into the world, she'd travelled once or twice with her eldest, then with the two older children, to her adopted country. But as for her island, I don't think she returned during that period. I even seem to remember that, in those troubled times of civil war, the frontiers were closed. And that, to complicate matters, having acquired French citizenship through marriage, she'd lost her original nationality—which, by the way, being careful not to make a claim, she didn't recover when it was again possible for her to do so. Because this restorative and licentious visit probably never took place, I take this malicious piece of gossip to be pure calumny.

If this adultery was ever committed—she was capable of it—it could only have been later, and perhaps it would have no longer been adultery.

According to her daughter: as soon as the frontiers were reopened, she went to her island to introduce her children to Es Predi, their grandfather, and Sa Predina, their grandmother, whose welcome of the recent widow and her three orphans, showing up haggard, dishevelled and without resources, was less than warm. They, also bled dry by the fratricidal war and the bereavement, bitterness and famine following upon it, no doubt feared they would have them on their hands. But there was nothing to fear. The French Army watches over her loyal personnel like a mother and soon was going to take care of the needs of these hapless souls. As for the recent widow who, we imagine, fulfilled without overwhelming enthusiasm her duties towards her old parents and young children, she must have burnt with impatience at the idea of returning to Paris—to roam its fashionable quarters, to stop in one perfume shop, then another—and especially to throw herself into the arms of her future second husband.

If one must, in the end, lend belief to rumour, it could only be then, offended by her family's reticence and confined, at loose ends, on this island where she found little enjoyment, that she might have given way with a distant cousin, vaguely resembling her beloved son, to an unseemly flirtation.

In spite of everything, I hesitate to give credit to this notion which at least has the merit of freeing her from the suspicion of adultery—of which, personally, I couldn't care less. She loved being seductive, that's certain, and constancy was not, young woman that she was, her primary virtue. Francis paid for that. But it just so happened that she was violently taken with her second husband—the legend relates—from the first glance, from the moment he'd caught up his violin to serenade his comrade's wife when he'd been invited to their house. I was, and with good reason, neither a witness to the birth of their love nor to the chance circumstances of their liaison, but I was present during the lingering demise of their marriage foundering, slowly, in sickness. To the wife's tragic decline when it was evident that her lord and master no longer recognized her, would no longer ever recognize her. To her ominous despondency when she was told that he was no longer.

And there's this foolish regret that she has formulated so often, and without the least sense of modesty: of unfortunately not being able, because of the late age at which they met, to attribute the paternity of either of her boys to him. Her words thus stung her daughter doubly, by revealing, first, the disdain in which she held her children's father, then, the primacy given to her sons.

It seems then that the rumour ran its course. Can one be surprised that a son, even if loved to distraction, shares a vague family resemblance with a distant cousin? And what does it matter to us if she did or did not dally with that cousin, since no damage resulted from it? Lastly, has anyone ever seen the birth of a child—and ten years premature!—due, at the most, to a coquettish glance?

What exactly did Francis know about his wife's repeated betrayals? Did he suspect that in introducing the handsome Jean into his household he was tempting destiny? But perhaps he preferred donning the suit of the obliging husband rather than the one she'd dressed him in for a time, that of a trusting spouse whom it was public knowledge she had deceived. And was it before or after he met Suzanne, the gentle quadroon, whom, at the moment of his death, he hoped to embrace as his lawful companion?

Francis and his young bride's honeymoon did not last long. Certainly he had applauded her bravery, saluted her courage when she gave birth to their first child. And he was infinitely grateful to her that it was a girl. Moreover, the success she was certain to have as an exotic Spanish woman, incongruous here, flattered him. But he had rapidly grown tired of her complaints, of her ceaseless recriminations. As for her, she must have imagined the climate of the colonies more mild and her husband more affluent—which he would eventually be—but she was impatient. Perhaps she also dreamt of a child more docile. Indeed, from the moment she opened her eyes, the little girl couldn't have been more turbulent—one might say that she has stayed that way if it weren't a bit indelicate to attach such an epithet to a woman now approaching sixty.

Francis, who spent his childhood exclusively among women—mother, aunts and a few neighbours, widows or those living alone, by the grace of what has been called the 'Great' War—devoted himself to them with a passion. Not to the generic, transcendent Woman that Don Juans, misogynists and other scoundrels make a pretence of celebrating to absolve themselves of the contempt they profess and practice in private, but to women, innumerable, industrious, ordinary, regardless of their age or attractiveness. It was from these simple, unassuming women who had wiped his nose and cleaned his rear that, convinced of its relevance, he possessed a fervour shaped by respect for the female race in its entirety. He'd seen them, mother, aunts and neighbours, not only watch over the children, keep up the house, mend the clothes, feed the chickens, tend the garden—without forgetting the tedious laundry sessions at the wash basin, the preserves in the pantry—but also scurry between vineyard and field, plough, sow, prune, gather the hay, harvest the crops, the grapes, carefully make and negotiate the wine, with only their two arms to do the work, and those of their like, belonging to a sex reputed, in spite of all, for being weak. He'd witnessed their open rebellion when the men, having survived the butchery and returned to their households more or less diminished, claimed they could divest them of their rights and limit their freedom. They'd protested loud and strong that, even as widows, even alone—the army, in its benevolence, having deprived them of their sons' support in order to give them a better education than their fathers would have—they'd shown they could stand on their own two feet, govern their land and their destiny. Francis' mother was of that calibre. Up until her death—she survived her son by more than twenty years—she ran her farm and her vineyards with a master hand, accepting from the village men only those services which she could remunerate, deaf to advice and disdainful of suggestions that others persisted in offering.

I see her, an old woman, almost a fossil for me, proudly perched on her motorbike—the only concession I know of that she made to the modern world; she did without a refrigerator, a radio, drew her water from a well and heat from a fireplace—calling whomever she pleased a *couillon* or *couillonne*,* according to the sex, in a stentorian voice that made me tremble. I knew the insult was banal for the women of Périgord but it offended my ears and turned my cheeks crimson. Why she never remarried, I have no idea. It's been said that she took occasional lovers from among the farm workers and her distant relatives but nothing of a nature to provoke the slightest legend. She neither bragged about it nor concealed it. That was life, *couillonne*!, as evident as the wind, the sun and the rain. Her legend emerged from her strength, her endurance, her stubbornness, her independence.

Her legend was to have given to her son, with his birth, the masterful lesson of her life. It's from her example that he derived this biased—but I want to believe lucid—enthusiasm, that of a proselyte, for what defines a woman, an enthusiasm that has come down through the generations. He, unfortunately, did not have the leisure to verify the accuracy of his convictions.

That's without doubt why Francis manifested so much patience, so much indulgence with regard to a sullen and inconstant spouse. His flighty companion's indecent behaviour in no way lessened his certainties, confirmed them rather: she was bored and made a fuss, but found a remedy! He simply regretted that her manner somewhat lacked in elegance. He would have appreciated more discretion, less alacrity in publishing her good fortune, which, for the most part, was found in the company of his comrades. And adultery was a common practice, at that time, in Saigon. The oppressiveness of the days encouraged it, and the gentleness of the nights. It's probable that he, too, conformed to the custom. He had a double reputation to defend: his virility, perhaps discredited by his wife's betrayals, and his gallantry, inherent in his status as a French officer.

But the legend—questionable, at times, I agree, from an over-zealous desire to be kind or the need to simplify—endows him with tastes, more modest, less venturesome, less perverse and less sophisticated, like boating at Cape Saint Jacques or furniture-making in the room he'd reserved for himself—to preserve himself?—in the domestic wing of the house. The race for a lover, we're told, was mostly confined to women, left to themselves, idle, a prey to vague dissatisfactions, to listlessness. They opposed each other in fierce rivalry. And capriciousness was the rule. Extra-conjugal escapades offered relief, were a luxury, prestigious but, in the end, of little importance to the men, solicited by their affairs, preoccupied by more serious questions than the strategies and fabrications concocted in the closeted world of women.

The legend has retained of Francis nothing more than the clear-cut image of an upright man. As for Suzanne, it was, above all else, a question of love. He was waiting for the end of the war. He'd given his wife's hand to Jean. His only concern was for the future of his three children.

I know of only one photo, and a minuscule one at that, where the entire family is united. I had it enlarged. What it lost in clarity it gained in eloquence. In the centre, the brood, framed by the two parents. They're seated, like cabbages in a row, on a stone wall that's too low to be comfortable. They're posed stiffly. Near Francis, the daughter, under the half-amused, half-tender gaze of her father, tries to assemble her too-long extremities. She has heaped her too-long arms on her too-long legs and clutches her elbows with her hands to hold the ensemble together. She wants to be proper, wants to please him. As she's fidgety and ungainly, and he likes to joke, he's in the habit of entreating her to gather in all of *that*— meaning her legs and arms—so that it doesn't trail about. She takes the criticism seriously. She'll need to grow taller by a few centimetres and older by a few months before she understands the innuendo. For the moment, she tries her best to oblige.

Near the mother, sprawling as he leans against her, the beloved son. Whenever she's present, he's there, glued to her side. He moves in her shadow, clings to her skirt and screams if someone makes a move in his direction.

29

He also screams when she goes to her room to rest or to change. The legend seems to imply that the child screamed perpetually. This couldn't have been altogether true.

In the middle of everyone, the younger brother. He's no longer a baby but, in contrast to his siblings who were not so much thin as skinny, he's plump. His face is round and his ears stick out. He's already bent over even though he's only four or five. He's the only one who's enjoying the occasion. His sister is petrified by her desire to maintain the correct pose, his brother preoccupied solely with claiming his mother's exclusive attention. The photographer is most likely allowing himself a few jokes. The youngest one, enchanted but puzzled, seems to be waiting for a bird that will fly out, by and by.

It's that this child was born credulous. His age has nothing to do with it. His nature is to blame. During the fifty odd years that have passed, it's been proven over and over again. He's remained quick to tumble for every last tale, to be delighted with the most tired of jokes, to let himself be fooled by the least cunning of rascals. Everyone agrees that he's both difficult and endearing, for the same reason and at the same moment. In his company, one is sure to meet up with catastrophe or, at least, run into bad luck, but one is also sure to break into laughter at every turn, not so much because of what he says but because he says it. The youngsters aren't wrong when they make loud demands for his crack-brained nonsense and his buffoonery. I must confess that he has charmed me as well, and charms me still.

Without the help of his sister who, very early, revealed the penchant that all deplore in her—because it has never failed to complicate her life—of sheltering the forsaken, dogs, cats or hominids, of taking on the defence of the innocent, preferably the ingenuous or simple-minded, I don't see how he would have found his place in this family, pervaded by two unique children, their father's daughter and their mother's son, which an open hostility opposed. Now and again, to the chagrin of his older brother, he must have succeeded in capturing his mother's attention. He was, after all, a boy, a potential man, regardless of appearances. But it just so happened that his sister, in her enthusiasm for their father, was more open to communicating. And as he wasn't devoid of the same feeling, she was taken with affection for this naive and vulnerable younger brother. How many times was she spied, armed with no more than her school bag, swooping down on a band of children that was cruelly teasing the little fellow whose only riposte was to sob, fastened to the two fingers he'd stuck into his mouth. And later, during the simultaneous ordeal of defeat and mourning, when they would be stranded, detainees or refugees, the legend has never elucidated this obscure question—in a sinister regrouping camp, it was she who would take care of him, depriving herself of some of her meagre rations to add more to his, putting him to sleep on her self, ridding his back of bedbugs and other vermin that were terrorizing him, while their mother devoted herself to the well-being of their brother, perhaps already confusing him with the image of the lover, disappeared, a prisoner, whose fate obsessed her.

It's with the title of 'little brother', and through his sister's benevolence, that he found a place in the family. If, as orphans, he suffered less than his sister—but, it goes without saying, eminently more than their mother's only son; the younger brother has lost all memory of his early years—it's because she protected him, and, when misfortune struck, took it upon herself to replace the father whom they both adored.

As for their father, he viewed this curious offspring, in whom he had tried to instil the rudiments of common sense and a few rules of correct behaviour, with astonishment and indulgence. From what they say, he sensed, under the surface of the incorrigible dreamer, the temperament of an artist. And he was right. But prevented by destiny to complete his teaching, this enterprise was only a partial success. The painter has a good hand and a firm manner but talks about working more than setting himself to the task. The man is gracious but changeable and naive, always late, incapable of providing for the most modest household. He goes through life unruffled and content, with no thought for tomorrow, always ready to party and to enjoy himself—rendering him pleasant company—always ready, also, to neglect his word, to avoid obligation, to burden others—making him seem like the plague.

And the plague hit early. Wasn't he discovered one day—but how old was he?—twisting the necks of a flock of ducklings in the middle of the farmyard, ecstatic yet, once his crime committed, slightly disappointed? The legend, perhaps exaggerating, gives us a count of twenty-seven. It appears that he in no way understood what the thrashings administered by the Bep, sa Ti—but what was the third nursemaid's name?—and his father meant. Even today, when someone brings up the incident, which he remembers no better than the rest, he expresses doubt as to its gravity. To the person who risks a reminder that provisions were short, Indochina being strangled, then, by the war, he retorts that it wasn't he, after all, who had declared it. Unbeatable indeed.

I won't go into details but his entire existence has been of a piece. Inattentive, awkward and credulous he was, and so he has remained. I'm a witness that, in this regard, the legend has added nothing to the simple facts.

As we know, Francis had little inclination to be part of the social set. Neither must he have been overly enthused by his wife's coquettish behaviour during their evenings out. It was not long, undoubtedly, before he renounced accompanying her to those dazzling soirées that pervade the legend.

During her frivolous days—it was different, apparently, after Jean entered the scene and she spent more nights waiting for him than making a display of herself at elegant receptions—they were the centre of her existence. She would prepare herself, at great length, when night fell and the heat of the day finally gave way. She bathed, perfumed, dallied in front of the mirror inspecting her make-up, arranging her hair, changed her dress a thousand times, then her shoes, all the time complaining, loud enough to be heard by the entire household, about the meagre jewels concealed in her modest jewellery box.

That, also, she would remedy but later, in the confusion that followed the Japanese offensive. She would take advantage of the occasion, entering—I wish I could write 'furtively' but that would be to romanticize and

distort, especially since I'm not unaware of the extent to
which she was governed by such impulses; it was almost
innocently, and without taking excessive precautions,
that she surrendered to this indelicate behaviour at a
nearby residence, emptied, like the others in the vicinity,
by the panic of its inhabitants. She would walk off with
the rings and bracelets of that one friend who was, from
time immemorial, the object of her most insane jealousy.
They would discover her offence. They would cry shame
and would single her out. She would face the uproar
draped in her dignity, hoisted on her high horse, not forgetting, however, to plead her recent widowhood so as
to halt the investigation and suspend suspicion. Only
when they'd disembarked in Marseille would her children understand why in the camp, then on the boat,
she'd taken such pain in arranging her hair. It was due
to this probable theft, hidden under the wide band
round her hair, that she had made sure of having the
superfluous—rice powder and Cuir de Russie,* a perfume much in favour at the time which surrounded her
with heady waves of odour, long-lasting and assaulting
the senses—when they lacked the necessities. A crisis
would force her to pawn them but she would not neglect
to reclaim them and, for the rest of her life, had the
immense satisfaction of adorning herself with them.

One ring, especially, heavy with its weight in gold
and bristling with myriad rubies, was, though rather ugly
and overly laden, her pride and joy. Was she telling the

truth when she asserted, though no one had thought to ask her, that it was the last present given to her by Francis, which, all the same, no one remembered?

In spite of the uncertain origin of this ring, it represented, for his daughter, the ultimate and, in fact—with the exception of a few photographs which I suspect might have been sent to Périgord, as a memento, at the time they were taken and recuperated later—unique relic of her father. Everything that belonged to them had disappeared during the turmoil. They had been repatriated to France, rich with nothing but their clothes, those that they were wearing at the moment of their departure, and of the little that their pockets could hold—and that the hair band could camouflage! Francis' remains, left to the care of the Japanese, are buried—at least that is my hope—somewhere in the outskirts of Saigon. And as for the grave dug in Périgord, it displays nothing more than a marble slab inscribed with his name.

Was the mother conscious of her cruelty when she used this ring in her attempts to arrest, with increasingly mediocre success, her daughter's rebellion? She nurtured her desire, then disappointed her hopes, sometimes promising to bequeath it to her, at other times threatening to disinherit her of it. But never did she have the faintest idea that she could simply give it to her. The blackmail lasted for years. Its effects were dulled over time. And it has been a long while since the daughter has stopped laying claim to this doubtful legacy.

The controversy over the jewellery would have been brought to an end long ago, with the statute of limitations, if, at least for one of her three children, there didn't remain—and I'm told that it would have been better not to disclose this doubtful episode of the legend, when, up to the present, I've not been reproached for either my irreverence or my plain speaking—the searing memory of, on the one hand, the indignity they'd suffered in public and, on the other, of their naive credulity before the vehemence of her denials.

At the end of her life, when she still had the power to move about but had fewer and fewer moments of lucidity, she acquired the habit of locking everything away—but really everything: linens, clothes, papers, crockery and, sometimes, even edibles. She would, to be sure, lose the keys, having hidden them away too carefully. That was, no doubt, less an effect of her derangement than it was the result of the aberrant lesson she had gathered from her experience.

It must, after all, be admitted that she has always been what one might call a kleptomaniac and that 'the jewellery affair' was not her first attempt. Nor the last.

We were aware of her weakness for lustrous fabrics and garish objects as well as her unfortunate tendency to appropriate them. When our exasperation granted us some relief, we would poke fun at it. One glance from her was sufficient to warn us of our imminent dispossession. And we would accumulate obstacles. Most of the time, in vain. She was as ingenious as she was perse-vering, which is most baffling, for she could have laid claim to what she coveted, and we would have gladly conceded it to her—did our willingness diminish her pleasure so much?—and most distressing, for she didn't in the least enjoy that of which she'd *relieved* us, as she would bury it, hidden from view, in the deepest recesses of her closets. We would point this out to her when she was caught in the process, but to no avail. She would deny everything and become angry. Then would grow faint.

As far as I'm concerned, inclined to be more indul-gent by the distance in time and space that separates me from her, I attribute this shortcoming, which seems more like a compulsion, to the miserable conditions, material as well as emotional, which presided over her childhood, compounded by the shock she'd experienced on arriving in France. She was not yet twelve years old and, at that point, had never left her island, or even her village—in front of the shop windows abounding with a profusion of food and goods and which overflowed from her godfather's stalls as well.

She would confide in me one day that she had felt like an indigent—and out of her mouth, that word had the ring of an insult—in her relative the grocer's house and that she'd sworn to herself that she would not remain one. Indeed. But her days of splendour as a thirty-year-old would last only a very short while.

Regardless of how strange it was, she didn't appear to miss them, though she took pleasure in recalling that time, but like a beautiful dream that had slipped away. The implication, for me, is that the presence, at long last official and legitimate, of Jean at her side had entirely gratified her, in spite of the fall from her pedestal and the ruin of her hopes. She loved luxury. But she preferred Jean. When one understands to what extent she was constantly agitated by her thirst for pomp and glory, one can only bow before the depth and the power of this prodigious passion. Unfortunately, even Jean, prodigiously alive, had failed in diverting her from her obsession, in curing her of her detestable mania.

And this defect I associate with another one, a morbid curiosity, for an analogous reason—without knowing how to justify this intuition—unless it's that she also wanted to take possession of our little secrets which she may have supposed more astounding than they in fact were. Did she fear that she had none of her own?

I remember the time, no more that a dozen years ago, when I came upon her in my study, on her knees, rummaging in the waste basket, carefully unfolding all the crumpled papers. I felt ashamed surprising her, and in a humiliating position. But she burst out laughing, as if she had just played a fabulous trick on me. And, once more, I admired her capacity to turn a situation upside down, as well as the astonishing elasticity of her values, and their scale, which has always disconcerted me.

Caught filching, she would cry out at the injustice, would sham a mortal affront or would faint. Caught nosing about, she was amused by it. And her victims, though irritated, absolved her.

In the vegetative state to which, from now on, she has been reduced, there is nothing more to fear. And we all deplore it.

There are no grounds for doubting that her deafness posed a serious problem for her, although for a long time she made a pretence of putting up with it, even turning it to good use. Her pride, easily bruised, must have suffered from it, but she refused to be accoutred with a device that was simply too unattractive. In former times, hearing aids were indeed conspicuous. Not easy to regulate, they would start whistling at the slightest mishap. She knew it, and feared less the annoyance than the ridicule in society. It was only in her seventies that, assured, not without difficulty, of the discretion of a modern apparatus, she resigned herself to wearing it, to humour us, when we came together for a meal. But she was accustomed to living in a haze of sounds. Noise tired her, the sudden din of the world round her, the clang of dishes, the roar of laughter, the squeak of chair legs—everything that henceforth she heard. Her eyes grew weary. They lost all expression. And her last companion, who loves her even more than she loved Jean—that is to say, with as much veneration but more concern, with abnegation—didn't wait very long before turning off the troublesome device.

As I've never succeeded in convincing anyone at all of the uselessness of raising one's voice when speaking to her, that one needed only to catch her eye or to alert her by touching her arm, these meals quickly turned into pandemonium. And we would leave this tumult extenuated and voiceless. Just as we had in the past.

This said, no one understood why, though clearly deaf, she was strangely selective in her deafness. Frequently she intercepted remarks that were not directed to her or from which we tried to exclude her by lowering our voice and which, perhaps for this same reason, must have attracted her attention. A very long time ago, I took great joy in pronouncing the forbidden 'word-of-Cambronne',* as she said, with modesty. Not once did she miss hearing it. Yet I was on my guard, waiting until either she, or I, had our backs turned. Nothing helped.

She could scold but, here, remained virtuous and set an example. I never caught her uttering, at least in French, the slightest vulgarity. Her language was polished, with a scattering of Spanish expressions, but with an extensive vocabulary, though many words had personal connotations. She'd derived her language less from imitating those like herself than from the scores of books she had consumed. She read laboriously, out loud, following the words with her finger, spelling those that were unknown or complicated. She delighted in reading *Angelica* and *Amber* and other serial novels, in spite of being almost illiterate. Destiny, unkind from her birth, had not permitted her, except ever so briefly, to sit on a school bench. If she had had the opportunity and the time to learn more than the rudiments of the alphabet and of arithmetic, it's likely that her existence would have been less problematic and she less dependent on the whims and, more particularly, on the fate of men, especially on that of her spouses. She loved to please, certainly, but she was independent—though perhaps not, she couldn't bear solitude, she needed a companion but one to whom she would dictate her wishes and who would submit to them, as it has happened with the last one. Her face must have flushed red often—I mean from rage or frustration, she seemed impervious to any private shame—for having to make certain concessions. And she was intelligent. She had a sort of intelligence that suits the situation, that expresses itself in the instant and that astonishes by its pertinence.

In the darkest period of her life—thus she qualified not the months that followed the death of Francis, amid the chaos of war, the terror, the misery of the regrouping camp, the humiliation of returning, crammed together, without amenities, on an overcrowded boat, confronted with the despair of at least two of her three children, but the years of mourning, of privation into which she was thrown at Jean's disappearance—better educated, she would have had access to that flattering status of lady-in-waiting, about which she so liked to boast—or to something better—and would have supervised her employers' households rather than execute their orders. She detested everything that related to keeping up a house. Sweeping, cooking, ironing overwhelmed her. She had done too much of that when she lived with her parents and her godfather, the grocer. At the very most, shopping offered a diversion because she conversed with the shopkeepers, the clients, embellishing her past, and because she spent money which gave her a feeling of importance. An immense injustice had governed her fate. She was convinced of it.

Prematurely retired, she had to return to the island she abhorred, though I don't understand why. Perhaps painful childhood memories were attached to it. Perhaps its inhabitants had knowledge of her Indochinese splendour and her affluent Parisian life only from patchy and disputable gossip—she avoided any reference to her reduction to the rank of a domestic. She feared that, for them, she'd remained the daughter of the owner of a shabby tavern, located in a distant suburb. In any event, this withdrawal to her native land, imperative for economic reasons, was a source of deep bitterness. Though by nature joyful and lighthearted, she fell into a depression as a result of it.

It was then that, happily, she met her last companion. She was approaching sixty, he was at long last a widower—and not in the least respect her cousin!—after having spent three decades caring for an epileptic and senile spouse. He had not had a life, and she wanted to taste life once again. In order to please him—he displayed a pronounced inclination for the blond hair and round forms of Marilyn Monroe; she, it goes without saying, fiercely jealous, didn't spare the star already definitively risen, nor her silhouette, whether animated or on paper—she had bleached her hair, which wasn't especially becoming. With that, she fulfilled one of her dreams as well. Her previous husbands had preferred her austere, dark beauty, which held nothing strange or exotic for her last companion, born in the same village, on the same island. As for the rest, she conceded nothing to him. And the time came when he was obliged to request a transfer, to accept exile, not to flee from her, as Francis did in times past, but in order to satisfy her wishes. Thus, she was able, for a few years, to continue to roam the streets of a large city on the continent and to devour the contents of its shop windows—a city that by no means equalled the hub of the universe. Frequent and sudden fugues to Paris followed, with, as her only luggage, her purse and the ugly cloth bag she used for doing errands. Her last companion complained that she never gave him warning: home from work, he would, one evening, find the house empty; he would wait for her a moment, then go off in search of her, hoping that she had lingered a while chatting with some neighbour—which was her custom. At last he would understand, become resigned, and worry until she returned. He knew that he had no means of preventing these escapades but asked for a little consideration, if no more than a minuscule message, 'In Paris,' or simply 'P,' left on a corner of the table. When he protested, she proved to be both deaf and mute. If he insisted, she would become angry or act like a martyred child, which softened his heart. It has only been several months since he's had the last word. He has not got over it.

When the hour of retirement sounded for him, the couple, illegitimate, were officially united by virtue of the proper authority. She had made the most of her excellent pension—and her admirable frugality—to have a house built in the better section, on the port, transformed to her great joy into a spot eminently suitable for tourism. And it was with her head high that she could finally regain her island, on the arm of the man who had redeemed her honour and who was, as well, her faithful knight.

To return to her strange selective deafness: the piece of bravura that the legend relates thickens the mystery. I can understand her knowing how to dance. Younger, she must have had better hearing and, in those days, it was the musicians who conducted the ball. Orchestras enlivened the dazzling soirées, which followed one upon the other in the 'white city' of the Beautiful Colony. The sound, which made her ear drums vibrate so weakly, no doubt diffused and resonated in her chest, in her body, when in proximity to the instruments. As she was graceful and loved the feeling of abandon when in men's arms, she followed her cavaliers' twirls without difficulty.

But that she knew how to sing the popular songs of the time—on key and in French—to the point of being invited to perform one evening, accompanied by Jean and his violin, on the waves of Radio-Saigon?

We could take it for a flattering invention of the legend. That's not the case at all. There are living witnesses, her children, permitted to stay up that evening, gathered round the crystal set. They listened, stunned and ecstatic, to their mother's performance, then to her triumph to thunderous applause. Until not long ago, they took pleasure in recalling it to her. She would promptly rise from the table and with a high-pitched voice—considered distinguished in the thirties and imposed on women but to us, today, seeming nasal and forced—would strike up a few old songs of which, in general, she had forgotten most of the verses. Invoking her age, she would apologize, not without false modesty, for these regrettable lapses—which deprived us from tasting to the fullest such undying masterpieces as 'My Tonkinese Girl' or 'China Nights'—and for her thin voice. But, in the end, she sang, and on key.

It's different for her daughter, though she's subject to the same impulses whenever one evokes the same memories. It's not unusual, when the discussion turns to Indochina and her childhood, to see her spring up from her chair and throw herself, arms extended, into a more or less faithful interpretation of the sinister: 'Maréchal, nous voilà!'* She's no longer among us. She's ten, eleven years old again. She's over there, yesterday, parading down a boulevard, whose name I've never retained, to celebrate Joan of Arc Day. A holiday when, at the height of her glory, as well, she found herself chosen to represent her school to lay a wreath of flowers at the foot of a dignitary, or perhaps of the statue, I no longer remember. Our bursts of laughter, each time, bring her back to earth. They surprise her and, in spite of what she says, irritate her. It's that, over and beyond the ludicrous incongruity of the situation, she can't carry a tune to save her soul and mixes up the words. Our hilarity ruffles her feelings with regard to only that. For the rest, she knows that she tends to relive what she is relating. A thousand times, in the enthusiasm of telling her stories, she has knocked over glasses, broken dishes, or worse, and she has no trouble laughing over it. But she prides herself for having belonged, at a period more recent than the legend but just as irrevocably past, to an obscure trio that did morning shows in a drab cabaret—it's not to be doubted, a photograph stands as proof, her charming face must have compensated for her off-key singing— and she doesn't appreciate our discrediting this flattering episode of her history. One can be hurt for indeed the oddest reasons!

However that may be, by a baffling whim of fate, the mother is deaf and sings on key; the daughter hears but is painfully lacking a good ear.

But how did the mother learn those tunes in which she took such pride and that so delighted her admirers? The radio or the gramophone must, it seems, be excluded. She didn't perceive sounds that were jumbled; we know the radio waves often had interference and the records crackled. Someone, Jean or one of his brief pred- ecessors, had probably gone to the trouble of teaching them to her. And perhaps she was talented. But, in that case, why did she keep that strong accent which stayed with her, as pronounced as ever, up to the end? At times one wasn't quite sure what she was saying. And there were all those words over which she stumbled. 'Mirilen!' she would cry out, in defiance, when she saw the object of her latest hatred appear on the screen or on the cover of a magazine. And 'What a Denis' she would comment when she passed an athletic-looking man in the street, something that troubled me for a long time. The Denis in question didn't in any way seem to merit this unappealing name. But all became clear the day I discovered, hidden in Denis *Adonis*, an image that enchanted her.

More easily explained was the reinforcing of her deafness in troublesome or uncomfortable situations. It was at times annoying that she made use of it without discernment, and against those close to her, but it would have been unseemly to compel her simply to submit to her infirmity. It wasn't unreasonable for her to obtain some benefits from it, rather meagre ones compared to the unpleasantness it caused her. Concerning this unpleasantness, she didn't say a word. She couldn't hear. Period. It was up to each to take note and to accommodate. She appeared to suffer less from that than from her Hispanicism. Was she hiding, or suppressing, her embarrassment and her regrets?

From this pain, silenced or denied, perhaps came the need she felt to assure herself of men's homage. As a young woman, the legend tells us, she was inclined to play the role of the languid femme fatale, with a touch of playful frivolity to give spice to her character. With advancing age, she abandoned a measure of seriousness.

And it was playing the mischievous little girl that she secretly conquered her last companion who, while she was slipping into dementia, no longer hid his treating her like a doll, tying her white hair with a pink ribbon, dressing her in sky blue or pale yellow, she who had loved nothing more than the quiet elegance available at Trois Quartiers: grey suits, neat blouses, discreetly embroidered, matching gloves, shoes and handbag, straight skirts, preferably of dark, tightly woven material. It was her pleasure to dress in such strict attire but she wore it to the last thread—curiously less for reasons of economy than to assert its solidity, the excellence of its quality, and to prove to the eyes of the world the justice of her predilection for a store as old-fashioned as it was expensive—and she put on weight, with the result that, after several years, the knit tops became stretched and baggy, the silks had runs, the seams split. There's no doubt that the Trois Quartiers, forewarned, would have declined this fervent publicity.

The legend, however, has preserved the memory of the sumptuous apparel with which she adorned herself when she went to a soirée, especially to the most dazzling of all, the one that consecrated her presence on the waves of Radio-Saigon. What was she wearing that night? A filmy ball dress of silk muslin? A shapely black gown, enhanced by a discreet diamond brooch? A blouse fitted at the waist over a flowing skirt of rustling taffeta? Or, still more troubling, that dress made of angel's skin, which clung to her body and revealed its every movement?

These garments, and others, left her children speech-less with admiration when she would appear, ready at last—after the countless hesitations and the litany of complaints with which we're familiar—at the top of the staircase that she would descend slowly, so as to judge the effect on her sons, who were suddenly overwhelmed by jealousy, and on her daughter, stirred by anger and envy. It was thus that she was announcing to the boys that she would be going out—and the beloved son would start to scream, soon followed by his younger brother who would make do with whimpering, less out of conviction than to join in with the older one—to the girl, that her mother would, without doubt, be compli-mented and perhaps flirted with, something that was unbearable to the daughter, more for her father than for herself.

This mother and daughter have never ceased con-fronting, provoking, losing all patience with each other. A dog and cat, one might call them, so much did they persist in repudiating, in denigrating one another. How-ever, in many ways, they were alike. Or, more precisely, their conduct, their comments—as antithetical as they seemed: the daughter's outlandishness was an affront to the mother in her obsession for respectability while the mother's egotism exasperated the daughter's exuberant and somewhat impulsive generosity—proceeded from the same imperious thirst for life, from the same stub-born revolt against the injustice of fate. Yet there was one thing that came between them—that insoluble rivalry, that is to say, their shared femininity. The mother was plagued by the thought of seeing her youth, her beauty supplanted by her daughter's. It was inevitable but she was never successful in resigning herself to it. In her seventies, she still boasted that men's glances were turned her way at dinner parties. And she never missed an occasion to congratulate herself on her perfect legs, which were indeed slender and shapely, on the beauty of her complexion, on the youthful appearance of her face where her weakening vision no longer discerned the slightest wrinkle. As for her daughter, she did not forgive her mother for having been an unfaithful, then renegade, wife—it's true that, at times, she pretended to have forgotten it, or perhaps it was the dementia that was already overwhelming her—of the only man that the daughter has ever revered: her father.

Not a concession, not an indulgence, from one or the other, until these last few years when illness and decline have got the better of their hostility.

The mother's impatience with her daughter, scarcely born, had not escaped Francis. For a time, he found this nervousness natural in a young woman, disconcerted by her first baby. He endeavoured, as best he could, to comfort his wife—but in vain: the child's turbulence wore out her patience, as did, even more, her skinniness which offended the legitimate pride of a Mediterranean *mama*—and to pamper the *phenomenon*, since, they assured him, a *phenomenon* she was, and they were not far wrong.

And the apprentice father, stupefied, observed the precocious burgeoning of the two fundamental attributes that have orchestrated his first child's life: an overflowing enthusiasm and a spirit of perpetual rebellion. He would have been delighted—it was the intrinsic vitality of women, and their perseverance, that he so admired—if he hadn't soon been forced to measure the extent and the complexity of the problem that these 'prodigious' gifts created in the family household. He, alone, and, to a lesser degree, her Ti Aï benefitted from her radiant ebullience, a necessary, but not sufficient, condition for her potential obedience. As for the mother and, for some unknown reason, the Bep, they were

treated to a permanent revolt, both vigorous and insolent. The tears, the cries, the crises, on all sides, followed
one upon the other. And Francis, an unwilling witness,
failed to pacify his little world.

Later, the mother's insistence on maintaining her
daughter's animosity by unjust and constant criticism,
then, the hoped-for son at last having arrived, the per-
ception of her obvious lack of interest had discouraged
Francis from attempting to arbitrate. He became resigned
to a life of tumult.

Meanwhile, he had adjusted to the status quo, which
gave him the elbow room to bring up the little girl as he
saw fit. In reality, he'd never had complete confidence
in the pedagogic talents of his wife, ever a Spaniard,
who manifested, in a manner well-nigh atavistic, a pronounced penchant for the masculine over the feminine
and displayed the most profound disdain for practical
obligations—with the exception, of course, of judiciously
choosing what to wear, where to go and who to take as
her lover!

With regard to the education that girls should have,
Francis wasn't devoid of either instinct or ideas. Both
were needed to check the disorderly exaltation of his
indomitable adventurer. Didn't he have to scold her furi-
ously—and all the more so because he had to smother a
smile—the evening she'd come home, crestfallen, her left
arm hanging limp? He had driven her to the hospital
that same morning to set the fracture that was already

on the right arm! He didn't restrain himself from poking fun, while she was convalescing, at the flapping of her flippers. Following this, he'd put his revolver in her hand and taught her to shoot. Did he harbour the insane hope that, rather than paying with her person, she would thus know how to defend herself from the world's unceasing adversity that her boldness and her want of foresight would, without fail, attract? He mistrusted, and with reason, her impetuosity—still more worrisome in time of war, even one still muted—but he couldn't fail to recognize her notorious clumsiness. Happily, she never had the occasion to exercise her expertise.

And it's with her body—as well as her soul; but no one, aside from me, has been allowed to utter even the hypothesis—covered with sores and bumps, that she has gone through life up to this day. Under her assaults, all, or almost all, the ladders have slipped out of place, all, or almost all, the chairs have broken a leg. Her fingers, though more than capable of concocting an exquisite meal, of improvising incomparable garments out of velvet or silk—the one is her art; the other, her profession—have been crushed by hammers; pliers, pincers, or any instrument at all harmful have been sharpened on them. The soles of her feet have been stabbed by every rusty nail, every piece of broken glass. Or almost every one. To say nothing of automobiles that, from the start, have declared her their enemy. In one of her oh-so-rare flashes of lucidity—at least with regard to tinkering with and manipulating machines—she saw that she was not up to the struggle and she resolved to condemn them to the miserable pile of unemployed metal—one of them still keeps watch, like a regret, deep in her garden, serving as a den for all sorts of rodents. Its doors squeak pitilessly in the night wind, but that's less of an annoyance. I must admit that this haughty disdain delights me. I know there's no point in anticipating, even well into the future, either, from her, the slightest progress or, from old wrecks, unexpected kindness.

Francis would get up early. She would, also, to take advantage of his presence before the house woke up and to share 'like sweethearts'—as he let her describe it—his breakfast. She used to wait, seated on the bottom three steps of the staircase, until he made up his mind to discover her there. As for him, he pretended to have his coffee, his mind elsewhere. 'Sun hat or umbrella?' he would, before long, fling out at her. And the formula's shorthand—it was about her mood, not the calm or menacing state of the sky, that he was inquiring—charmed the youngster as much as its daily repetition. Thus, when they were alone, she answered, invariably, 'Sun hat!'

The moment would come later to take out the 'umbrella' for protection from the storm let loose by her brothers or her mother, her classmates or her teacher, if it wasn't from her own incapacity to accomplish some feat, to secure a favour, storms that were devastating but that passed quickly. A caress from her Ti Aï, a bantering smile or a knowing glance from her father, along with the noisy despair of her younger brother frightened by her violence—the baby brother, that is, the tears of their mother's only son, when they didn't exasperate her, left her indifferent—were enough to calm her.

Her anger cooled as abruptly as it had flared up. With a pout, she was silent, turned her back and walked away, putting on an air of nonchalance. Before long, she was bored with sulking. She took note of the blue sky or the brilliance of the bougainvillea. She was not yet out of sight before she recovered her liveliness, her carefree spirit.

Resentment she has never known, or bitterness, which is more surprising at her soon-to-be sixty years of age. Perhaps she was never one to relish sadness, to mull over morose thoughts. It seems to me, however, that it was more her father who dissuaded her from such feelings. He was jovial and inclined to scoff when he met distressed souls and mournful faces. Something of the child she's preserved within her—as everyone has, but, with her, more acute, her childhood having ended, irremediably, at the death of Francis, before his mutilated corpse—has never stopped wanting to please him . . .

The news has broken: the son, the one so loved, is dead. He has just died in a hospital on that other continent he had, indeed, chosen and in which he'd vanished.

What exactly happened? And how is it that, knowing he was sick, and perhaps mortally so, he didn't consider renewing relations with his mother, if only by way of a few words hastily scribbled on a postcard, like that laconic farewell he'd sent some twenty years earlier from a stopover in India to signal their estrangement? He knew the address where it was certain one could, within time, always find her, the one for Es Predi's house.

Despite the trouble this decrepit house caused her, she had never wanted to part with it, undoubtedly for the very reason that its address was known by everyone, that it in some manner represented the family seat, a kind of anchor in their tormented lives where one day a letter, awaited so long and in vain, would perhaps arrive.

Having returned to her island, she would go to the Calle Ozonas each day with a vague and futile pretext which fooled no one. She'd climb up to the attic, search in the old trunks, come upon photos or bits of letters and start to cry. About Jean, or about her beloved Claude—he's dead,

*we can call him by name without fear of doing him injury
—that is to say, about herself, her past.*

*Little by little, in her afflicted and perhaps already
clouded mind, the idea took hold of making this almost
hovel into a palace for the return of the prodigal son. At
first, she'd forbidden anyone to enter, excepting her last companion who was allowed nothing more than to drive her
there and wait patiently on the doorstep. It was no longer
possible for anyone, even just passing through and for the
night, to make use of the place. Later, she generously invited
us to admire the construction, but we were authorized to
observe the progress of the work only from the half-open door
which she held with a firm grasp. The metamorphosis
accomplished—and Es Predi must have turned over in his
grave with horror, the sober flagstones of his tavern covered
with modern tiles, as hideous as they were glossy, his rough
walls that, in former times, he took care to wash with lime,
smoothed out by a layer of plaster, tinted with lively, 'stylish'
colours that went well together—she occupied herself with
furnishing it 'luxuriously'. She proceeded, as if in a ritual,
in this house that had become a temple, where she would
come to reflect, secretly lament and revive memories. I don't
know at what moment she became aware of the affliction
that was going to do away with sanity. Never, perhaps. Her
age, simply, in an unexpected moment of lucidity, would
have suddenly worried her. Or it might have been her last
companion who, fearing a disaster, strongly encouraged her
to do it. In any event, at more than eighty years of age—
and scarcely a few months before the attack that was to*

cast her into darkness—she resolved to make out a will. To Claude, she bequeathed the house. From then on, she changed nothing. She limited herself to passing by every day to pick up the rare pieces of mail, all unrelentingly administrative.

Claude has been gone for several weeks. She, pitiful wreck, remains afloat on the agitated sea of her interminable approach to death.

But it suddenly occurs to me: it's possible that, victim of an accident, stranded, dying in a far-off hospital, he didn't have the time to put things in order. At present, no one can tell. Only one letter arrived, at the above-mentioned address. It emanated from the French embassy in Sydney with an information form to be filled out by, and about, the family of the deceased. For what purpose? One dares not think. This news fell like a stroke of lightning. It devastated those to whom it was sent. With the single exception of the mother who will, I hope, be spared, regardless of the state she is in, the searing pain of the unacceptable: the definitive disappearance of her child more than dear to her, on foreign land that will be, forever, unknown to her.

It was a mistake—I perceive it now—but it seemed to me that I'd never felt the slightest stir of tenderness for this curt and haughty person. I remember, at most, having appreciated his bearing, which, like Jean's, was handsome but which, like Jean as well, he owed to the air corps and to the prestige of a flattering uniform of which he was quite proud.

From early childhood, he'd shown a marked penchant for the military, its pomp and its discipline. His mother liked to recall that hardly had he heard the flourish of the army bugles—and parades followed upon troop inspections in this idle time of undeclared war, the Colonial Army ruffling its feathers to rouse the troops, impress the locals, fool the enemy and, incidentally, enthral the youngsters—he would dash into the courtyard, arm himself with whatever he could find for a rifle, an old, worn broom, devoid of its 'feathers'—he, so caught up with his idea, unaware of how ludicrous it was—and would start marching. The legend specifies: under the marvelling eyes of his mother, the indulgent ones of his father, the approving ones of Jean, the amused ones of the servants, the resolutely furious ones of his brother and sister, hardly in favour of either this monkey-like behaviour or this playing the actor and stealing the show. The youngest brother had tried, once or twice, to fall into step with him. His sister took it upon herself to discourage him.

Unfortunately, he did not make the air force his career due to an accident on take off, from which he escaped alive, but not unscathed, his scull held together with plates of metal. The latter, according to his brother and sister, didn't contribute to improving his character. Being shunted aside, more than the modesty of the pension, had mortified him. It rang the knell for his hopes of a soldier's glory.

The rest of his destiny gets lost somewhere between the quicksands of the legend and nasty gossip. After the failure of his first fugue—we know in what way, with an expulsion that he considered ignominious—he'd returned to his studies. Written a thesis, the legend says. Nothing more than a kind of certificate, one of the most vicious tongues around has whispered with, regardless of the legend, no lack of arguments. I have no way of judging, having seen him very little during the last days of his stay in France. And it hardly matters.

In contrast, I had some knowledge of his talent—criticized—to collect women as well as stamps, fiancées, as people would say modestly and out of consideration for the children who might be listening. But his brother and sister were not deprived of their own fiancés in great number and just as fleeting. Thus, it wasn't the fact in itself that displeased but the objects of his choice and what he wished to attain. He surrounded himself, preferably, with women who were as stupid as they were blond, who were in raptures over his muscles and his athletic exploits. In a certain manner, he paraded, as he did before, and without respite, before his troop of geese, armed with his broom!

The 'Sun, Sex and Sea' which, they say, prevail in Australia must indeed have fit him like a glove.

Except that more than twenty years had gone by, that he, like everyone, had grown older and, perhaps, changed.

We know now. Claude died of leukaemia. And, the irony of fate, the request for information was designed to take a count of his inheritors. In this instance, only his mother, since he seems to have remained, there as well as here, without a spouse or descendants.

Poor mother. Poor solitary heir who, happily, remains unaware of it. She, who so loved money, would have been at a loss over what to do with this dreadful succession. That, at least, would have been spared her, as well as seeing her name—she'd kept Jean's—badly spelt on the envelope that the embassy sent her, and the address of the palace, the temple—the anchor—on which she'd staked so much, almost unreadable and incomplete. Proof, if it were needed, of the little importance that, for years, she'd had for Claude. He had not seen to registering his home address. And it's on a yellowed piece of paper, torn from a notebook, put into a folder without an indication of date or contents, entrusted, in times past, along with others, to a lawyer—for safe keeping? or as a good way of ridding himself of them?—that the name and address were found.

Until a very short while ago, the date of 9th March—
1945—brought to my mind only Francis' heroic march
towards an uncommon death. Nurtured by the legend,
I never failed to celebrate this anniversary of a private
disaster which overwhelmed the destiny of an entire line
of descendants and afflicted the orphans—whether or
not they know it or, for the recently deceased, might
have known it—with a dull uneasiness and a singular
instability. Indeed, all three have left their country, several times over. And she who was most affected has
proved herself the most roving.

I was unaware that Francis' martyrdom was only a
minute motif on the immense fresco of a massacre.

The legend, however, has never glossed over the war,
neither its horror nor its fury. Much to the contrary. It
treats it like an earthquake, a hurricane, like an eruption
of the elements to which one submits, terror-stricken
and powerless, from which one emerges, devastated. One
cannot take our legend to task for not giving history its
due. That hundreds of soldiers had been executed that
night and that thousands of others were imprisoned, it's
not that it didn't remember—it's that it didn't see, didn't

really know, blinded, anesthetized by the breaking of the tidal wave. It merely gathered up, after the storm, the wreck that was Francis, dead, and the account of Jean, disappeared, a prisoner.

It's from this private catastrophe, in a shattered universe, that the legend derives its power and its long life. Without this wound, which was not healed and, therefore, suppurated since that baleful day in March—the indissoluble pain and memory, unaltered—our dear but, after all, banal legend would have turned sour like so many other impoverished chronicles. In time, outworn, then resolutely obsolete, it would have slowly smothered among yawns of boredom, emptied drop by drop of its substance, to the point of testing the patience of the protagonists themselves. But Francis, phantom member of a nebula, its head amputated, has never ceased to haunt it, to torment it.

History, in all its majesty, should have come to the rescue of our faltering legend and granted me its clear vision. However, here, in metropolitan France, and over decades, a very curious amnesia has reigned. Total silence—troubled?—with regard to the Beautiful Colony of times past, indolent and winning, inhabited by gracious Annamites.* Hatred, choked with rage, for the bloodthirsty plebeians—henceforth referred to as 'Viets' —and their ungrateful dependency for which they'd just laid low our valiant troops, messengers, nevertheless, of peace, liberty and progress. And I didn't know where I was in this inextricable labyrinth composed of two unexplained wars.

The lead cover finally cracked, slowly letting in light. Prompted by the passage of time, offences were pardoned. Unless one owes this precious knowledge to the presence, once again, of an unreliable nostalgia. In any case, it was in the leaves of books that I discovered, only recently, the missing piece of the enigma that, in spite of everything and forever, Francis will remain for me. That is to say, his premature death, at thirty-five, wasn't the price of a flamboyant defiance, of a sublime bravura, but, rather, the sinister issue of a pitiable wartime strategy: that our wondrous hero had, along with others, been above all a victim, certainly courageous but sacrificed.

That evening, his daughter had accompanied Francis to his barracks. She was proud to carry his basket containing a change of clothes and clean sheets. Francis—though it wasn't in his nature; it was going to be his turn to stand guard—was grumbling. He was sick and tired of the army, of its discipline, of its impeccable white uniforms. He grumbled all the more since, at this point, he could no longer elude events. If this cursed war hadn't been declared, he'd have treated himself to many a tranquil day in *pékin*,* as a peaceful civilian. To think that he'd carefully prepared his retirement—he had, in fact, started a factory or, rather, a workshop, for furniture that he loved to make and, notably, had acquired a small grove of rubber trees of which, in any case, he would have been plundered at the end of the Second World War, and even if it had turned out, after all, to be advantageous for the French colonials, he wouldn't have derived a profit for long, synthetic rubber, as we know, having triumphed over green gold—it had been at his fingertips. But there you have it. In the heart of old Europe the unacceptable occurred, the irreparable had been committed: France, not yet subjugated, was defeated; its army, not yet disarmed or taken captive, put to flight. Francis had resigned himself to prolonging his service which his painstaking sense of honour would, in any event, not have permitted him to evade.

But that evening on the way to the barracks, in front of his daughter, he was grumbling. His complaints are the last words that she heard from him, along with his order, when the shooting started, to run to the house and not turn round.

How could Francis have underestimated the danger to the point of risking his favourite child's life that evening? For months, books inform us, the tension had been increasing. The Japanese, we're told, had become more and more numerous, more and more present, less and less civil, in both senses of the term. It's not possible that Francis, with the grade of a non-commissioned officer, was unaware of it and, as a prudent father, would not have taken it into account. His mind was, perhaps, elsewhere.

It's true that both of them took pleasure in these moments of intimacy and easy conversation, far from indiscreet ears. His daughter, who was growing up, approaching adolescence, we imagine, with difficulty, confided in him her heartaches, her resentments. He shared thoughts about their future, dreaming, in a way, out loud of a serene remarriage with the gentle Suzanne, or about the organization of the factory, the running of the tree farm. They put a thousand plans together and at times argued over them heatedly. With regard to the place and the role the new wife would assume, he assured her Suzanne would never be an obstacle. More awkward was the question of where the children would live. He did his utmost to persuade her that it would be in their best interest if their mother maintained responsibility for them, preserved family cohesion, took care of their growing up and their schooling—she who could barely read, who cared only for the well-being of her beloved son, she who was preparing, once freed from the bonds of this mediocre marriage, to abandon herself entirely to her prodigious passion, then, victory secured, resume her frivolous, entertaining life and—who can say?—sing once again on the waves of Radio-Saigon, accompanied by Jean and his violin.

The young girl had no delusions. Thus she tried to negotiate a special status for herself, not hesitating to flatter unduly, praising the qualities of the gentle Suzanne or the virtues of a rustic life on their property. Francis found this manoeuvre, that of a child, amusing, but he did not give in. He justified, as he'd always been obliged to do with this obstinate but astute youngster, the sound reasoning behind his decision. She had to understand that she would be the object of everyone's reprobation. Whatever he might do, and though he intended to marry again in the most proper manner, he would still remain for all an *encongayé.** She was sensitive to the coarseness of the insult, without grasping the full meaning, and she didn't see what was even more dishonourable in the fact that Suzanne was a quadroon—in the eyes of everyone the fruit, already, of a misalliance. Her father's seriousness and the unfathomable stupidity of grown-ups put an end, temporarily, to her contentions.

She remained, however, something less than convinced of the necessity of living under her mother's roof and under the authority of the intractable *Tonton** Jean.

Under this title, the family had graciously opened its doors to the hapless bachelor. And he'd done his best to honour the confidence that was placed in him. In spite of the stinging remarks that Francis persisted in casting his way, his friendship did not slack. As for the wife, it would be legitimate to think that he was devoted to the friendship—although, later, one could speculate that this wasn't without its ambiguities. He considered the oldest child a calamity, and the immaturity of the youngest one overtaxed his patience. In front of their father, however, he showed nothing of what he felt. The older brother was the only one who was in his good graces. And with a strange effect of mimicry, they resembled each other: the same arrogant expression, the same stiff carriage. Moreover, he alone would agree to call him *Papa* when their mother remarried. It was only after abundant step-father slaps and abundant shedding of tears and maternal blackmail that the oldest one compromised, her little brother, as always, tagging along, and *Papa* Jean was benighted. But far from pacifying him, this reticent sur-render strengthened and justified his tyranny. To escape his ready hand and his malicious comments, the one found herself constrained to rush headlong into the coils of an early and disastrous marriage, the other, to seek refuge, before the call-up, in the ranks of a more-than-ever providential army. The *Tonton* that had preceded *Papa* was surely less malevolent.

As resignation, when she was a child, was not one of her most outstanding traits, the youngster, after a brief and thoughtful silence inspired by her father's sombre reflections, started up again, now even more eagerly. She created her own world where one would only have to think about boating on Cape Saint Jacques—with Suzanne, since he wanted it!—bike rides round Saigon or Bien Hoâ, interminable breakfasts, chatting together 'like sweethearts'. No more school, no more mother. No more brother—she was willing to admit the little brother into their circle. No more *Tonton*. No more reproaches. No more punishments. An eternal sun hat! Never again an umbrella. She rhapsodized. Francis smiled.

And a step away from the barracks, the bout that was to decide the outcome of the war was taking place. The Japanese won it, temporarily. We know with what consequences.

About Jean: Francis was accustomed to saying, with a malicious smile, that he was in the wrong army—had he known what we've known for a short time apropos of the army that Jean had mistakenly joined and which remains to be proven, at least in its implications, Francis would have been even more biting and certainly less confident, at least concerning his children—and he didn't spare his irony in the other's presence. Not that he endowed him with any guilty fondness for the midget, gesticulating Japanese soldiers. That would have been as ridiculous as it was unjust. But, even more ferociously, he scoffed at his obscure resemblance to the arrogant *Wehrmacht*, blindly disciplined, frighteningly efficient, without scruples or human feeling.

Jealousy played no part at all in this severe judgement—however paradoxical it seems, Jean's entrance on the scene had brought his wife's most flagrant escapades to an end and it was the lover who was from now the butt of her impatience and petulance—nor did the Alsatian origins of his rival and, nevertheless, friend, whose political convictions, it must be said, he shared.

It's that, indeed, there was in this man, Jean, something imperious: a cutting disdain, a latent cruelty, a cold calculation to which I can bear witness, although I only knew him late in life, already diminished by sickness.

Francis and Jean. They were very nearly the antithesis of each other. The one, from Périgord, massive but jovial, with eyes that sparkled. The other, Alsatian, a pleasant exterior but totally devoid of humour, with eyes that chilled. Try as we may, it's difficult to imagine their friendship. Yet they sealed it—not the least surprising—before a photographer, a professional one: their features are retouched, the photo is signed, correspondence card is printed on the back. They posed side by side in dress uniform. A medal is fastened to Francis' chest. Where did it come from? It isn't there by the photographer's whim alone. The legend, however, has not preserved the slightest trace of an intrepid deed that would have earned him a decoration. With the exception, of course, of his heroic conduct in the face of death. But he was recompensed for that posthumously.

Interesting, their mutual positions. Francis slightly dominates Jean who, in reality, was no doubt over a head taller, or more. Is it out of respect for a difference in rank? Of this I'm no surer than of their difference in age. I can only state, upon viewing this odd correspondence card, that they weren't in the same branch of the army. Their dress uniforms are similar but not the form or the placement of their stripes, which, as we know, are resolute in withholding any meaning for me. Or did Francis, distressed by his short height, ask to be raised up, as they did then, with one or two bricks, invisible in the photo? But I doubt that his modest height, not any more than his stoutness or the whiff of a provincial accent, ever really disturbed him. Didn't he want, rather, to play a trick on his comrade with this vain pretext, or even without his knowing, and place the hierarchy of their friendship on a moral plane, publish and signify to their correspondents—transmit, if necessary, to posterity?— his benevolent but lucid condescension?

According to the legend, this was a friendship made of interminable discussions where they systematically opposed each other. It must have been exhausting—and how they exhausted their companions, we're told—but it had an attraction for them since, up to the end, up to sending Jean on a mission to Tonkin, a few weeks before the fateful night, they didn't stop fencing, Francis growing purple with enthusiasm or indignation, Jean turning pale with rage or resentment. They agreed on one point only, on their secret allegiance to a rebellious general whose name they avoided pronouncing. It's perhaps the reason why, in spite of all else, they respected each other, for this shared resistance, however diversely motivated.

They, at any rate, disputed interminably, a hair's breadth from a malaise, inches from a duel, on those evenings when neither one nor the other was constrained to his respective barracks and when the lover, quite exceptionally, was not committed to chaperoning the wife of his conciliatory friend.

But she, what did she think of this barbed friend-ship? Exclusive as she was, she must have suffered from it, in default of blushing—for many a year, she'd no longer been mortified by the open knowledge of her furtive romances; it seemed to her that she had recovered her respectability with Francis' tacit, then declared, accord. The indifference that Jean, lost in the infernal circles of their interminable arguments, suddenly mani-fested couldn't fail to exasperate her. On this question, the legend makes no pronouncements but, since one more dab of paint won't change the portrait, I suspect that she, more than once, interrupted the dispute by way of a caprice or a pretence of feeling faint.

Less narcissistic, less infatuated with herself, she would have been disturbed by this curious friendship. Francis confessed without hesitation, when he was the subject of mockery, that he'd adjusted to this question-able companionship, one that at least relieved him of his marital or social obligations and that fostered intelligent conversation—and, without doubt, the upright citizens could only grimace when so amiably put in their place. But it would not have been in Jean's temperament, whose overweening pride and caustic tongue were noto-rious, to accept without wincing the insolent, and often hurtful, banter with which Francis abused him. This uncharacteristic passivity—whether he was fascinated or simply submissive—could have been the little birdie that told her, as could have been much of his later behaviour, disconcerting for such a prodigious and reciprocal passion. For years on end, she attributed Jean's frequent nocturnal absences to the constraints of his service. And she believed, unhappy thing, that she owed his negligence to the effects of his gruelling escape. All of which proves that jealously, morbid as it is, is no guard against betrayal.

How is it that she, jealous beyond measure, never suspected Jean's duplicity? To my knowledge, she never allowed him to go out alone, at least not in their part of the city. And each workday, she accompanied him to the train station and returned to pick him up, regardless of the hour or the season. I remember—when I was confided to her care and he was still alive—being abruptly awakened late in the night or in the wee hours before daybreak to go to meet the blissful husband. I'd be drugged with sleep, refuse to walk, stamp my feet, but nothing would help: we'd leave for the station. And he had only to mention an urgent errand or a letter to mail and she, nonchalant as she was, would put on hat, shoes and gloves in a fraction of a second. In truth, however, it must be said that she was bored to tears keeping house. Any excuse or occasion was a chance to escape, rub shoulders with the crowd, have her head spin from the lights and movement. Not quite in her right mind but otherwise still fit, she'd take advantage of the slightest distraction of whoever was watching over her to dash for the door and hurry away. In the end, upon the request of her last companion, weakened and overwhelmed, it was the police who took charge of finding her and bringing her back to their house.

One had to see her, anchored to Jean's arm, trotting alongside him, throwing irate glances at each woman passing by, ready to spring if one, or both, of her precious husband's eyes strayed in that direction. How many scenes did she provoke in the street? And in receptions! It was with design and utter perfidy that the lady of the house would place him next to her at table, separating one from the other, and ask his company for a waltz or a tango. She would boil in silence for a moment, then explode, denounce pell-mell the beginning of a plot, the wickedness of the hostess, the blindness, or worse, extreme kindness of the guest, her consort—and, from experience, she knew what it was all about—the scorn for her person and the lack of respect for her infirmity by the other guests. As a finishing touch, she didn't hesitate to take revenge on, here, a crystal glass, there, a porcelain dish, to the detriment of Jean who, at a loss, would drag her towards the cloakroom and the way out. She, who detested having her deafness even mentioned, used and abused it as a pretext whenever it suited her.

One had also to hear with what self-assurance she accused the postman, a prying neighbour or a naughty child, when she handed him his crumpled mail, in envelopes clumsily re-glued. And to catch her inspecting his clothes where, obviously, she never discovered the least trace of lipstick or blond hair.

More judicious, she would no doubt have spared herself the dramatic revelation dealt her on the way back from Jean's funeral, meant if not to console her, at least to assuage the violence of her despair, a revelation that she held secret or—much more probable—kept carefully buried for almost thirty years, that, one day, she shared with her only daughter when perhaps she was already losing her mind or when the worsening dementia had done away with this inhibition.

Her daughter, after almost a decade, remains dumb-struck and doleful. But, mad as it is, there's no need to cry wolf. Jean, without really trying, was the predilection of women. That, from time to time, he—and like so many others—preferred the company of ardent gentle-men, today, no longer scandalizes anyone.

With the proviso—unpleasant to contemplate—that he might have made use of Francis' wife and three chil-dren as simple screens. What his commander suggested to his widow on the evening of his funeral.

But Francis understood Jean better than anyone else. He was fully aware of his faults as well as his qualities. The acerbity and the recurrence of his sarcasm, inscribed in golden letters in the legend, attest to it without reser-vation. If he'd had the vaguest suspicion, not concerning his comrade's habits—in conformity with the period, he would perhaps have teased him but, more open-minded than most, he wouldn't have gone any further than that—but about the possibility of such a base manoeuvre

by his friend, it's certain that Francis, a responsible husband and a loving father, would not have granted him
his wife's hand so readily nor entrusted his children's education to him. And, in so doing, their destiny.

Since Jean had Francis' complete confidence, one mustn't, it seems to me, pay undue attention to this accusation levelled by his commander on the evening of his funeral. Regarding the revealed secret, not the slightest doubt. The benevolent army couldn't have invented a tale of such bad taste, and which hardly flattered it. It did nothing more than peddle the piece of gossip with the intention—laudable!—of allaying the widow's pain, not of harming her. But to accuse Jean of a vile and under-handed manoeuvre, that's another step. For my part, I won't take it.

It's on the fertile soil of a liaison extending over several years, and after living together for a few months during the difficult times of post-war Paris, that Jean entered into wedlock with Francis' widow. He'd had more than enough leisure to appreciate her supple character and her delicate manners. He lived yet some ten years at her side, before dying from the effects of his captivity.

This longevity, it must be said, is something of an exploit. Francis had shown less perseverance, cloistering himself in the servants' wing of his house. It's only her last companion—but he's a model of abnegation, provided with a constitution of iron and a will of putty—

who has succeeded in adjusting to her perpetual excesses of behaviour, and of affection.

From his death, deferred, but recognized as glorious, she drew her pride in being 'twice a war widow!' for which, as we know, she was repaid in endless red tape and vexations by the profuse—deceitful?—French bureaucracy.

For having suffered his capricious spouse up to his last day and for having smiled at her, still, in the throes of a painful death, it had to be that Jean was profoundly attached to her.

I might add that Saigon, at the end of the thirties, must not have lacked women who were more beautiful, more refined and less temperamental, who were, like her, promised—but, obviously, no one could foresee it—to an early widowhood by the malediction of the 9th of March.

All of these facts fly in the face of the deplorable allegation proposed, without undue precaution, by the nevertheless reputed Grande Muette.

And these too: I've seen with what tenderness he'd brush strands of her hair, unruly as ever, from her face, or take off her coat or extend his hand to help her up the steps to their first house—the only one, for him, deceased before the completion of the banal but costly suburban bungalow that he, dying, had resolved to offer her because she so desired it. I've heard with what infinite indulgence he'd respond to her perpetual questions, submit to her inexhaustible babble—she feared silence almost as much as solitude; that's precisely how, later, she wore out her beloved son's patience and drove him to violence, then to flight. And when her jealousy didn't provoke a scandal, she, herself, was the object of it because of a petty theft or a trivial indiscretion. If Jean, as it was claimed, had sole need of a cover to conceal himself, he'd have been wiser to ally himself to a docile being, an unobtrusive companion, a hearth cricket. Instead, he'd chained himself to a sort of rare bird, flamboyant, certainly, but tyrannical, and quick to take offence.

A legend, of mysterious origin, has arisen concerning Jean's enlistment in the army. It seems that, as a student, he wounded his roommate while cleaning his hunting rifle. And this veiled legend insinuates that it was perhaps not an accident but—in an undertone—an act of revenge or—with a knowing look—of despair. This last allusion—justified or not—seems to me too subtle, or at least, too precise not to have been elaborated after the fact.

If Francis is an enigma—partially resolved, but I'll never know the sound of his voice nor be able to confirm the veracity of his legend—Jean resembles a complex puzzle, with various solutions. From the manner in which I've chosen to assemble the pieces, a character emerges, torn, humiliated, in total and constant contradiction with himself. Torn between his mental rigidity, the moral—not to say the inflexible—rigour of his education and his secret penchants that this same morality stigmatized. Humiliated for being a slave to his senses, the plaything of his emotions. Moulded by society, he couldn't help but share its disapproval of dissidents of his sort. As for his cruelty, which surfaced in such a flagrant fashion, it's probable he exercised it especially against his person, mortifying or chastising himself for a supposed dishonour. And this impression of guile that his impassible traits and his frigid look produced, perhaps came from a permanent, and painful, strategy to keep temptation at a distance. Perhaps. Playing his violin, he seemed the most gentle, the most sensitive, the most refined of men. If not for the twists and turns of his story, and his combat lost in advance, I'd be willing to believe that he'd have shown this pleasant aspect of himself more often.

One cannot doubt the passion that Jean and Francis' wife felt for each other during the time in Saigon—though less prodigious than she imagined. Insatiable and flighty as she'd been—and would become again after her second widowhood, and even a little before, sneered some nasty gossips here and there, but who could, at that point, reproach her?—she wouldn't have been satisfied with a lover who was too distracted or distant. The children, it must be said, knew everything, or almost, concerning *Tonton*'s visits to their mother's bedroom. The only slap his daughter ever received from her father was for having the naivety—or the sauciness—to demand to know why they were forbidden to enter the conjugal bedroom when unlimited access was authorized for the blissful *Tonton*.

Neither can one doubt the tender solicitude felt by Jean for his ageing wife. The costly bungalow in which he knew he was never, or hardly ever, to reside, would in itself be sufficient proof. On their wedding photograph, he still bears himself proudly, filling out his chest, holding his head high to greet the occasion and honour his service for the medal and new stripes that had been bestowed upon him. In contrast, under her mantilla, she looks older than her not-quite-forty years. Fatigue and adversity are inscribed on her face, read in her eyes. But the legend, without pity, is categorical: it would be a mistake to discern traces of distress endured in the last year in Indochina. Her boundless egotism had, it seems, protected her, if not from fear, at least from an awareness of the irreparable disaster which had just struck her family and her adopted country. Of course she'd experienced the cries, the sweat and the blood, the terror and the sorrow of her three orphans, the vermin and the promiscuity of the regrouping camp but, according to the legend, she had traversed this chaos in perfect thoughtlessness—with the exception of the rescue and safekeeping of the rings and bracelets of her close neighbour!—Jean's disappearance being her only torment. She would send her daughter—and, here, we've stopped laughing—to identify her dead husband's body, the daughter, only able to identify her father's shorts, and never able to forget his cadaver, putrefying. Another time, horrified by the screams of a dying man, she would flee the trench where everyone had taken refuge, forgetting that she'd left behind two of her three children. And when Jean finally returned, but sick, extenuated, she would let her entire progeny—the beloved son included—wander through the devastated city, risk every danger, witness atrocities, like the junk with masts and sails gaily decorated, much like a Christmas tree, with men's heads, cut off—as she rushed headlong to the bedside of the dying man, moving heaven and earth to save him. By force of stubbornness, of ruse, of intelligence—she knew better than anyone how to manipulate her entourage, passing from the most arrogant insistence to the most beseeching entreaty, according to the circumstances, the authority or the competence of her interlocutor—by force of devotion, she would succeed. The unspeakable wife and mother revealed herself, on this occasion, to be an exemplary lover.

Jean had been captured, the same March night, in his remote Tonkin barracks. With some tens of his comrades, he'd managed to flee. I've only the vaguest notions about this epic escape. Jean didn't like us, in his presence, to allude to it, and we all respected his silence. What little I do know is that they'd made their way for six months, moving only at night, and that Jean had seen a number of his companions perish, poisoned for not having, like him, the will or endurance to eat nothing but hot peppers and drink nothing but rain water, gathered from the surface of leaves. He owes to the irreversible ravages of this diet the cancer of the digestive tract to which he'd succumb twelve years later. But after this welcome reprieve of twelve years. And it's handsome as a god, though swollen from scurvy, his blond hair floating on his shoulders, that our sometimes lyrical legend relates he entered Saigon, not long delivered from under the yoke of the Japanese.

Is it after this trial—either that having lived each day side by side with death had put the priorities of his existence into perspective and reduced his sense of guilt, or that this rare and harsh experience had softened, but only relatively, as we've seen, the rigidity of his character—he'd become resigned to being himself, but being it honestly? Was it before? Or still later? No one will ever know.

Jean may have finished his life in the throes of a lie and in fear of treachery, but he preserved the serenity of the woman he loved, kept his word to his friend and yielded, without any further hypocrisy, to his true nature—which seems to me to be lacking in neither bravura nor virtue. There are acts of fidelity that are more absolute than those simply of the body, vulnerable and inconstant. She must have known that, or have sensed it intuitively. That's why, for almost thirty years, she hid, or buried within her, this staggering secret.

Ever since I've been old enough to think for myself, one question has tormented me: How could a mother be so cruel as to delegate to her daughter, still a child, the task of identifying the remains of her deceased husband? Was she that oblivious? Or cowardly? Certainly, there were rumours concerning these mass, and summary, executions. And as for the Japanese reputation for savagery, it had been amply confirmed. Surely she must have suspected that the horror of the scene would add to her child's pain, to her despair? All the more since she couldn't be unaware of her daughter's mad course through the streets of the occupied city, showing to each passer-by, whether French, Annamite or Japanese—and a god exists for mad orphan girls, the Japanese, then, not showing pity for anyone—the photo of her father she held clasped in the hollow of her hand.

How long did the family remain without news of Francis? A few days? A week? Several weeks? And who informed them of his execution? His commander, I suppose. But the legend, more poignant, affirms that it was a Japanese, an officer to boot, and immensely tall—if there were only one, he was destined to be the messenger of our unhappy legend—who was said to have bowed, in the wife's absence, to the daughter, too stunned by the strangeness of the situation to be frightened, and to have barked in a stilted French: 'Mademoiselle, it was I who had the honour of killing your father.' *The Honour—of—Killing—your—Father.* So be it.

With honour, or without, Francis was most assuredly dead. From nineteen bullets into his body. And finished off by the slash of a sabre from the top of his head to his middle, stopped in its thrust by his shorts, the remnants, perhaps, of his pants. That was the fate reserved for the hero who, listening only to his courage, had put fire to the arsenal and blown up the ammunition.

I now know why, for years, I believed in a heroic deed, exemplary—which it was—but isolated. An intrepid initiative. An insolent, unique act of defiance. It's because of this legendary Japanese.

I'd of course heard about the Nipponese offensive, about the terror and the rout in the first hours of turmoil—so accommodating to the cupidity of Francis' wife—about the frenzied flight from trench to trench, under fire, the screams of the dying, the cries of a wounded man, invisible, calling—as in the poem*—for a drink; about all those anecdotes which denounce and authenticate a state of war, no longer muted but declared. Our fabulous hero, however, seemed to me to have thrown caution to the winds, meeting these contingencies head on, the sole person to have seized the standard of revolt and, with a grandiose gesture, defied the enemy powers. This immensely tall Japanese officer bowing, humbly, before the orphan, recognizing both his crime and its tragic necessity—before such bravery, which was an honour to him, the murderer—this legendary messenger could not be a part of the base, warring multitude. Thus, when I pictured the scene, it was endowed with a mystic aura, like an Annunciation but inverted.

This said, behind the edifying figures of the fabulous hero, of the weeping virgin, of the announcing—as well as the exterminating—angel, the raw images have never stopped taking shape of a swollen body, alive with worms, wearing shredded shorts.

For what reason was Francis, like his comrades, denied a proper burial—the legend, tetanized, has no memory of why. Their only fault was to have been in the wrong place at the wrong moment. For which they were penalized more modestly by expeditious decapitations?

I would like to believe, in spite of everything, that this burial was only postponed, and that Francis' remains were indeed entombed in that land where he'd chosen to live, in serenity, for the rest of his time on earth.

As an example? To kill the germ of a possible rebellion? But the French were annihilated, the escaped military captive and the civilians penned in under secure guard. As for the native inhabitants, they surely did not intend to rise up against those who claimed to be freeing them from under their colonial tutelage.

For vengeance? To glory voluptuously in the crushing victory? From pure barbarism? But the barbarians' nose must also have been insulted by the stench of the half-decomposed cadavers.

I know that in time of war, in the delirium of slaughter, such delicate feelings are not tenable. I know, above all, that it would have been far better if the child had been spared this atrocious spectacle, which, fifty years later, still returns to haunt her nights.

Certainly, the Japanese are to blame. They share a collective guilt. The exterminating angel, less than the others, for having soothed the orphan girl's heart by invoking his *honour*, which raised Francis to the Olympian heights of a fabled hero. But how much more guilty is the unspeakable mother?

I would like to have learnt from her mouth that, sick or whatever, she'd been prevented from assuming her role, obliged to delegate it, by the force of circumstances, to her eldest. It was nothing of the sort. Concerning her first husband, the father of her children, she never said a word. Later on, she all but forgot that he'd existed. Already, for a number of years, she'd denied her children the ability to remember him, as well as the radiant and prosperous times before the war—with the exception of her triumphant performance on the waves of Radio-Saigon. I don't know what happened to the beloved son. As for the youngest, he, in fact, remembers nothing. Not his father. Nor his Ti Nan—that was the name of the third nursemaid, his own, which, by chance, came back to me. Nor the flock of ducklings strangled by his good offices. Nor the taste of Chinese soup. Nor the regrouping camp. Nor the wretched crossing for the return. The first ten years of his existence have toppled into a void. As the subject is, for him, fearful, one can suppose that it's by this amnesia that he's preserved himself from the shock wave that ravaged his sister's soul and, less enduringly, her body.

She wasn't yet twelve years old. She had lost a father she'd revered. Was it under the escort of the Nipponese angel that she made her way to the barracks—I don't dare question the legend on this tragedy; under the words one still perceives too many tears—barracks on the road to which the two accomplices had so often debated, plotted in secret? We know what she discovered. She saw the shorts, they were indeed her father's, and smelt the pestilential odour of death. Two of her senses saturated with horror, repugnant with disgust. For the sense of hearing and of touch, it was over. Never again would she hear his teasing voice. Never again would she turn round and throw herself into his arms. Her childhood had blown apart.

The nightmare, ushered in on this strident note, would be unrelieved. It seems to me that, over and above her childhood, it was her very reason that would have blown apart if, instinctively, she hadn't transferred all the affection of which she was deprived onto her younger brother. Is that why he never really grew up? Because of this overflowing love, resolutely blind, of which he has benefitted well after his young age, even today, in spite of his debonair and irritating buffoonery? She'd taken upon herself the duty of serving as a relay of their father's presence, of being the remedy for their mother's perpetual lapses. To have charge of her brother, in a time of torment, would save her, if not from despair, at least from its immediate detonation.

It's only upon returning to France, and after having borne a thousand affronts—'In Indochina, they called me *the noodle*,' she'd say again and again to her classmates who would burst into laughter over such ridiculous boasting, totally unaware that in Indochina noodles were reputed to be lively and those that emulated them, quick, audacious—after having suffered the scorn harboured towards those from the colonies and their misfortune, more or less suspect, merited, in a way—the State had too many wounds to dress and rounds of pleasure to catch up with to be upset by the drama that had been played out in the Beautiful Colony and by its pitiable destiny—that she was to collapse, devastated, both her legs paralyzed.

Bone decalcification, due to the privations caused by the war, was the diagnosis. Perhaps. But not exclusively. Because it was on her two sturdy legs that she descended from the boat in Marseille—and after fifteen months of terror, of mourning, of penury, and thirty days of the harsh crossing that's been related—on her two sturdy legs that she stayed in Périgord with her paternal grandmother—who, without fail, would bellow out *couillonne*! when she stopped in her tracks, frozen with admiration, or with a more aching and obscure emotion, before the hills and woods where Francis had romped as a child; 'You'll see,' he'd often say to her, 'how beautiful France is, its singular seasons, its subtle, always varied, light;' he'd omitted to specify 'its rude winters and its freezing rain'—on her two sturdy legs that she'd entered the boarding school. Yet, it was on a stretcher that she left it.

Nothing in the legend about this. Nothing confided to anyone either. Just one fact, unembellished, that, for decades, I've struggled to elucidate.

That the deferred detonation occurred in a sinister boarding school—and I know from experience what boredom, loneliness, sordid and gratuitous vexations these places provoke—doesn't appear to me to have been coincidental. Separated from the only being of importance to her, isolated in a hostile universe where no one understood how she suffered from the cold, her clumsiness—all thumbs when using a knife and fork, having always, from her childhood, preferred chopsticks that, in contrast, she employed with dexterity, though no one in the school gave it a thought; and she wasn't in the habit of moving about bundled up in thick and heavy clothes—where no one excused her distraction, what she claimed to be momentary confusion, the orphan had, without a doubt, withdrawn within herself, allowing the wheels of the 'little bike' to spin free, the one that, sometimes even today, 'circles in her head'. Memories of the happy years. Boating on Cape Saint Jacques. Walks in the vicinity of Saigon or of Bien Hoâ. Joyous breakfasts together, 'like sweethearts'. Free and easy talks on the road to the barracks. But also shots, cries, panic, horror. Perhaps, in this infernal merry-go-round, she heard the sound of her father's voice entreating her, in that blessed past, gone for ever, to gather in *all of that*—meaning her legs and arms—so that *it* didn't trail about. And indeed for more than a year, they no longer did. She was bedridden, deficient—less of calcium than of love, of paternal tenderness—riveted to the spot from insane obedience, crushed from an excess of silent pain.

Fortunately, this wasn't the only recommendation, the only lesson in deportment that Francis had given his daughter. He'd followed their fancy, hers as well as his, in educating her. He was willing to play Socrates when they were together and demanded nothing of her of which he did not explain the necessity, outside of, from time to time, her silence, without much success, and a little discipline of her turbulent gestures, with a result that has already been noted.

His principles were as simple as they were definitive: a generous and pacific philosophy of life, an indomitable faith in the female race, lucid indulgence for the

weaknesses of humankind, compassion for the unfortunate and, inversely, a cheerful impertinence round distressed souls and mournful faces. Without forgetting:
audacity—but, for the present case, not much was lacking, one needn't be too insistent—perseverance and,
whatever turn the world took, respect for, and faithful-
ness to, oneself.

As he'd shown himself, on every occasion, to be playful, upright, noble, to the point of heroism, she had,
while he was alive, followed his example and, when dead,
transformed him into an ideal, a model for her con-
science. And it was to gratify his wishes, it seems to me,
just as it had always been, that from the depths of her
despair she'd collected herself, found the energy to get
well, the courage to stand up.

She often confesses to having only partially conformed to the demanding rules of conduct prescribed by
her father—though, with regard to the unfortunate,
she has never shirked mercy. Countless dogs, cats or
hominids, of every type and character, crippled with
rheumatism, ugly, stupid and, most of the time, infa-
mously parasitical, have profited from her generosity, the
two-legged ones having been, to no one's surprise, the
least inclined to show appreciation.

But Francis must have been only in part this perfect
man—he loved life too much not to have, from time to
time, surrendered to pleasure, lacked rectitude or civil-
ity—that the legend has consecrated.

Yes, the image is blurred of the woman called Maria—the wife of Francis, then of Jean, the abusive mother of her first son and the unworthy one of her other children.

Ever since I was born, I have wavered between tenderness and rancour in my feelings for her. Her nature fascinates me, the force of her character, the incongruity of her temperament. And her slips of behaviour have more often enchanted than appalled me—at least once the moment has passed by; at the instant, I would happily have fled into a mouse hole to escape the troubled or dismayed looks of bystanders or, when I alone was concerned, to conceal my embarrassment from her. Her gaiety, her vitality, her freedom from care charmed me. And, above all else, I appreciated her royal disdain of an orderly house: never did she keep account of whether I made my bed or put my things away. When I was under her supervision, she'd send me, to my utter joy, to the bar below, treating me to a toasted cheese sandwich, with, on the side, a beer sweetened with lemonade, tasting deliciously of transgression—I wasn't of age but that didn't disturb her in the least—while she finished her day's work with her illustrious employers. After which she'd come to join me and, into the night, the party would continue. We'd go off for a walk in the elegant quarters, the Chatelet, the Opera, or better still, we'd stroll along her cherished Champs-Elysées. She never grew weary of walking as well as of gabbing—which was more troublesome. She'd speak in a loud voice, unable to hear herself, and didn't spare commentaries to me about the build, the dress of passers-by or, as she wasn't devoid of imagination, on their possible relationships, with a marked predilection for stories of illegitimate couples, one-night romances, flighty affairs, without my knowing if she drew these inventions from her reading or from her experience. When I'd be wilting with fatigue, it would be she who would implore: 'Just a little longer, please!'

I never understood the pleasure she'd take in comparing prices, in sumptuous shop windows, of clothes, shoes or fancy baubles she'd never be able to afford nor, in restaurants, her detailed and interminable perusal of the menus,* when even before passing through the door it was certain she would order the intermediary one. Not the most modest one—at least not until she'd met her last, and parsimonious, companion—that looked poor. As for the most onerous, it wasn't within her means. She thus managed to deal with her pride and her pocketbook at the same time. She must have, in that fashion, nourished her dreams of opulence and of prodigality.

At any rate, at the hour we went walking, there was nothing to worry about: the stores were closed. And as for the printed menus, it would have been of no use to her to make off with them—though, on occasion, she did just that. For what purpose or reason? It remains a complete mystery.

It's that she also pilfered from shops—trifling objects, a second pair of gloves like ones she'd just purchased or an embroidered hanky, easy to whisk away and, above all, to justify: she was so absentminded; one couldn't doubt her honesty, since she'd already paid—but never in the world from the famous Trois Quartiers where she considered herself known and respected.

Respectability, the word always on her lips, was nearly an obsession. Something that is disturbing, surely, to those who remember the less-than-virtuous woman she'd been—and without undue remorse—as well as the cheating here and there she'd allowed herself. She was a bundle of contradictions.

One had to see how she flung herself into action to compel respect in my boarding school, where the staff, with the exception of the nuns, was exclusively composed of Spaniards. I was proud to have her accompany me—and hoped, I confess, for a little tolerance of my pranks and failings, sealing by her presence an alliance, in some way tribal, with the damned counsellors who persisted in trying to curb my ways. She was proud to accompany me there, to impress her compatriots by her remarkable conversion into a distinguished and experienced Frenchwoman. Each time, for both of us, it was the same disappointment. Just as she counted for little with them, so did I. Very much later, I learnt that, before travelling on the continent with her last companion, she spoke broken, laborious, Castilian—but the counsellors were, for the most part, from Madrid, from the miserably poor suburbs, to be sure, but from the Capital, as good a reason as any other to be pretentious!—and thus betrayed her insularity, a contemptible provincialism. As her pronounced accent in French didn't escape them either, she found herself discredited, in their eyes, in both languages. And I didn't collect the winnings I'd expected. But I suffered less for myself than for her who misjudged the motive for this deplorable lack of interest, and who induced it again and again, at each new visit, tangling herself up into a web with her efforts. At the end of my internment, I'd given up availing myself of—or, rather, what I considered were—her Iberian virtues which, far from being of service had, on numerous occasions, done me harm: as a member of the *clan*, or its, so to speak, equivalent—and the disdainful nuance was clear—I had still less of a right to incur disapproval than my fellow students. In fact, in every which way, I lost out. I had thus resigned myself, not without sadness or resentment, to do without both her person and her hoped-for influence. But that she wasn't rendered justice wounded me. It's that I loved and admired her. I admire her a little less but love her still, as one can see.

Except that I was never able to avoid an irrepressible desire to recoil when I was near her. The Cuir de Russie, which she drowned herself in, made me nauseous. And she had this mania, typical of grown-ups of her era—it's been a long time, indeed, since I've chanced upon this gesture, tender perhaps, but oh how humiliating, either among my friends and family, or even on the street—of wetting a finger or the corner of a handkerchief with saliva and rubbing my face energetically to rid it of traces of powder, ink or dust. I knew that her personal cleanliness was uncertain, not to say dubious—she has always detested water, even now she fumes with rage when one starts washing her, and passing a wet washcloth on her mouth or hands is enough to incite a string of piercing, outraged cries, where I think I've, on several occasions, recognized the sound of *no*—but that wasn't what repulsed me the most. Beyond a repugnance—natural enough—for another's saliva, I felt this gesture as an aggression, as an attack on my integrity, a raiding of my sense of privacy. And stronger yet coming from her who did it with a kind of frenzy, denying others their alterity. Of her flesh, I became her belonging, and she treated me as such. One mustn't suspect that, as a child, I was overly sensitive. Her daughter recalls this gesture with the same loathing, remembers the same inexpressible feeling of revolt.

It's that she was superlatively possessive and invasive—by now, quite clear. Apart, perhaps, from her beloved son, and only when he was a young boy—as well as, one can assume, her numerous lovers—everyone has always endeavoured to avoid her embraces which, it must be said, had all the earmarks of an attempt to suffocate.

She also had a special way, and especially exasperating, of furtively running her hand over the arms, thighs, buttocks or breasts—just as she did to her own, moreover—of women who came too close to her, whether relatives, friends or simply neighbours, as if to assure herself of their solidity, or to compare them, to their detriment, of course, to what she considered, up to the dawn of her decline, her towering glamour. As time went on, I forbade her to touch my breasts, which made her angrier than if I'd insulted or struck her. To take revenge, she would threaten to palpate me, a form of teasing, in bad taste, that was endlessly repeated. I've long forgiven her for it.

Her last companion—whom I didn't remember having met during my summer holidays in Majorca—still reproaches me for my insolence and lack of docility. He says that, in the past, he would have most willingly bestowed a slap or two upon me, amply deserved. I wasn't, I agree, the most pliant of youngsters, but she had the knack of getting my goat. It's that she was capable, at times, of being as juvenile as I. I'd have a furious desire, perhaps, for an ice cream or a pastry, but she'd have the same furious need for me to forgo my playing and join her for a walk and distract her from her boredom. And we'd squabble like two rag-pickers. She was no less capricious than I. She would stamp her foot in anger, or plague me, childishly, until there was an explosion. After which it was obviously difficult for her to re-establish her authority. Moreover, the example she offered with her pretences, lies and other sly sorts of behaviour wasn't always edifying but it amused me prodigiously. I interpreted these injuries done to propriety as joyous recreation. To sum up, in our fashion—and, if it may be said—we understood each other.

Where the shoe pinched, and pinches, is that I understood very early—too early undoubtedly—that she was the cause of a deficit, an instability, contagious, among her descendants. Whether she loved too much or not enough, she has always failed in her duties as a mother.

The beloved son she ruined from his birth, by her wild pride in the little male issued from her body, the object of her fantasy that, flesh of her flesh, and of the opposite sex, he'd remain faithful, tied to her until her death, whom she hoped to make her staff of support in old age, almost her companion, in case of necessity. And that's what she had attempted, after her second widow-hood, imposing on him her presence, her deafening chatter, her asphyxiating embraces—while he laboured to finish his thesis, or some kind of diploma, of little importance now—until, about to suffocate, livid with rage, he committed the irreparable gesture of hitting her and, frightened by his violence, guilty—one doesn't raise one's hand against a mother—but lucid—it was only once underground that she'd leave him in peace—he resolved to disappear forever on the other side of the world, to lose himself on a vast continent, in a gigantic country, and thousands of kilometres from its capital, in an industrial town, known only to an informed circle, on the obscure site of a uranium mine, uranium that would be fatal to him—one can legitimately incriminate this aggravating factor, given its basic toxicity, in provoking his leukaemia—uranium that would prevent him from arriving at the age where, it's said, old resentments are appeased and reconciliation is possible, at least in thought, with the one who had ordered his days, who had, in spite of everything, been, during the time of his childhood, the object of his exclusive passion, his unconditional admirer, the indestructible incense-bearer for his thousand and one little vanities.

It is known now that, warned he was mortally ill, Claude had refused to have his family informed. He feared, according to the nurse who cared for him in his last moments, that it would hasten his elderly mother's death—but what gave him this absolute certainty that she was still of this world?—and he didn't want to alarm his brother and sister. He wasn't indifferent to their being affected subsequently, but he preferred to maintain his silence to protect them, to free them from blame, since in no way could they be of help.

Less ungrateful, less implacable and cruel than one had accused him of being—it seems that, in his last years, he'd drawn nearer to God and, cut off from the world, lived in an isolated house with, for sole company, a horse and a cat—he had proven, in these terrible circumstances, confronting, alone, the horror of his approaching death, then his imminent demise, to have exceptional courage. And, sparing those close to him, if not the sorrow of mourning, at least the anguish and torments of a desolate impotence, he revealed a disconcerting magnanimity.

May we, here, give him thanks.

The youngest was also a son, her son—that is to say, a possible prey, and an easy one, for her appetite to dominate, an inestimable recourse in adversity, justified, as will be seen—which occurred to her only after her beloved son had disappeared, without leaving a trace, and been gone for several years.

Had he not chosen, this youngest one, to put down roots on the island, where the Mediterranean light and the innumerable fields of tortured olive trees appeared inexhaustible to his artist's eyes—and where, it must be said, he could, if need be, sponge off his mother, lodge in the house of Es Predi, and feast at a reduced price —he would, perhaps, have escaped from the tardy but firm maternal grasp. She encouraged his heedlessness, his indolence—thus she kept hold of him; it was give-and-take: a small bill in exchange for a service rendered or a concession to her whim of the moment—and was enchanted by his escapades, which gratified her pride, that of a somewhat misogynous Latin mother. Hadn't she retorted, with a toss of her head, when a neighbour complained about the assiduous frequenting, improbably platonic, by her son of a niece that was in her neighbour's care: 'You'd do well to stay home and look after your hens when I let my rooster loose!' Most eloquent, if not elegant.

This sweet and already almost old boy, a jokester, a dreamer, ever vacillating, was never fated to become a husband or father. She had to lead him by the nose. And the big goose had given in. After which she applied herself to convert his wife into the most loyal and the most resolute of enemies.

One easily imagines the inferno into which this little world has been thrust now that she lies, demented, bedridden and incontinent, secluded—for almost three years—in the bedroom of one of her grandchildren, if not at the expense of her son and daughter-in-law, at least under their charge, with the aid—and the encumbering presence, but he'd have been happy to do without this cohabitation, if his state of health had not imposed it—of her last companion.

As for her daughter, not content to neglect her, she was relentless in disappointing, in mortifying her. When she was still active—yet another feat—and I'll finish here with this part of the indictment: she succeeded in forgetting her daughter's departure for Germany where they were going to cure her paralysis, save her from despair. The child waited for her, in vain, alone—when the other sick people were surrounded, comforted affectionately—shivering on her stretcher in the glacial cold of a train platform, for her, unmerciful in its emptiness.

How can one reproach this daughter—when the irresponsible behaviour of her mother had characterized her entire childhood, in such a monstrous fashion, so persistent, so systematic and overwhelming—for her relative lack of interest and comprehensible disgust for the daily care, fastidious, unpleasant, that the dying person from then on needed? She has not eluded her obligation, however—though she shows less skill than solicitude —but, by sacrificing no more than her Sundays, she 'husbands her resources'. Not a one of her fellow helpers welcomes such clarity. And the inferno has attained its ninth circle in the soaring of cries, arguments and reprisals.

It was the 'twice a war widow', and so proud to be French, Maria who rendered her ultimate condition perfectly unlivable. She had only to recover her original nationality, and without jeopardizing the one she'd chosen, in order to have someone claim home care for her, or a bed in an institution. But nothing in Maria's life has ever been self-evident. And this hell of which she's the involuntary cause, of which no one knows—she less than anyone—if she's the victim or the beneficiary—it is, in spite of all, the loving faces of her companion and of her children leaning over her, hands, regardless of all else, compassionate and tender that care for her—is the last perilous turn of her jagged destiny.

She not only failed in her duty as a mother but in what she owed to memory as well. To my mind, that's perhaps more serious. And yet I've suffered for her not conveying to her daughter, through indifference, through negligence, the essence, the recipes for a serene, responsible motherhood—though her daughter would have made a remarkable father, very like her own, complicit, intuitive, joyfully unpredictable and always enthusiastic, but these are not qualities, be they precious and enriching, that one expects most often from a mother.

Regarding Es Predi and Sa Predina, Maria's parents, I only know what I've seen. And that's little. Of Sa Predina, I've the image of a tall woman, boney, dressed entirely in black, swaying back and forth on a rocking chair in front of the tavern, cooling herself with a fan, black as well, that she folded up with a quick flick of her wrist as soon as someone appeared on the street. It was thus that she commanded one to stop and pay one's respects. And her order was akin to a decree. She didn't like me. She disapproved of me, the fruit of an estranged couple. I incarnated a dishonour that she would like to have spared her house. She frightened me. And we didn't understand each other. As for Es Predi, who survived his wife by a few years—for me, a few summers—I have the memory of a sly, old man with a good heart. He, who claimed not to understand a word of French, would have fun surprising me, in a fit of anger or in a sulk, with a litany of various, and choice, insults of genuine, though old-fashioned, Parisian slang. And never without the desired effect.

I still smell the odour of anise which would escape from his glass demijohns that contained the diverse *hierbas* and *cassallas*, which punctuated the days of those who were more friends than clients. One used to say about him that he'd let 'grass grow under his feet'. I confess, in spite of my efforts, and to my great disappointment, I never discovered any sprouting on his tavern floor.

Maria never spoke about her parents. Her real life had started upon her arrival in France. She insisted we accompany her to greet her numerous brothers and sisters, as well as their children, but managed to stay only for an instant, using us and our busy schedule as a pretext—and, being an undisciplined child who couldn't stop fidgeting, I was particularly useful to her. She was not anxious for us to learn what she'd chosen to cloak in silence. I doubt if her secret was of any significance— the austere authority of Sa Predina and the flaccidness of Es Predi were notorious, their poverty evident— but she was fierce in maintaining it. She did her utmost to forget, to deny, the unlucky, the unhappy little girl she'd been. If only she had confided the nature and the particulars of her childhood suffering, we would certainly have understood her better and, more willingly, have absolved her.

For my part, it is only her cowardice in not facing the death of Francis, and her obstinate, scornful silence in his regard, that I'm unable to pardon.

Of Francis, all I shall ever know is what the legend has recorded. One voice with one song. At times lyrical: 'He wasn't handsome but he had charm, a look that was affecting, intense, eyes of a marvellous green, radiant with intelligence, sparkling with vivacity, unfathomable, mysterious, calming, of a disconcerting green, just as yours are'—and, for years, I've tried to convince the guardian of this legend that my eyes are of the most banal brown; I was obliged, in spite of everything—so as not to sadden her—to concede, on very sunny days, a vague golden reflection. At times elegiac: 'I searched for him, I searched for him for a long time, I ran like someone crazy under the guns and among the wounded, I held his photo in my hand, it was all wrinkled, and no one recognized him.' Sometimes epic: 'Suddenly an officer loomed, he was tall, you know, very, very tall for a Japanese, if I'd been the emperor's daughter, he wouldn't have bowed more humbly, and he said: 'Mademoiselle . . .' Sometimes a voice broken by tears: 'I saw the shorts.'

Francis, due to his brief existence, to his distant exile, to the gust of wind that carried him off, decimating his intimates, his allies, together with his adversaries, seems to have been spared by malicious gossip—unless it's the guardian of our legend who has erased, one by one, any trace of nastiness. It was not so with his wife. Not when she was. Nor afterwards. One cannot disagree that she exposed herself to it with an undeniable obstinacy, a pursuit of the incongruous, one might even say the scabrous. But her volcanic temperament, the simplicity of her loose conduct, her deafness, skilfully exploited, brought upon her, from the mediocre, the envious, a thousand spiteful acts of vengeance and unjustified anathemas.

From now on, in that land, inconceivable, forever veiled, where her spirit has preceded her body, she'll no longer suffer from them, and her secrets lie enveloped in silence.

Maria, my undeserving, my frivolous, my irresponsible, my capricious, my flighty, my iniquitous, my unfortunate, my extravagant grandmother, may she enter the darkness in peace.

La Grande Muette: literally 'The Great Silent One', an ironic reference to the army, sparing of information, and to the lack of freedom of speech for those in the armed forces.

couillon, couillonne: an insult in other regions of France but, in the Périgord, a term almost of affection.

Cuir de Russie: literally 'Russian Leather'; a perfume.

word-of-Cambronne: *merde*! (shit!)—what Pierre Cambronne (1770–1842), the French general, was reported to have exclaimed when summoned to surrender at Waterloo.

Maréchal, nous voilà!: chanted in honour of Marshal Philippe Pétain (1856–1951), head of the Vichy Government during the Second World War.

Annamites: the original inhabitants of the Vietnam lowlands in the area around Saigon.

pékin: refers to civilian dress.

encongayé: a man who lived with an Annamite woman, who was called a *congay*.

Tonton: affectionate term for 'uncle'.

poem: refers to *La Légende des Siècles*, a major poem by Victor Hugo (1802–85).

menus: in France, most restaurants propose a choice of dishes 'a la carte' or grouped in 'fixed-price' menus.